T0194702

RESTRAINED
JUSTICE

RESTRAINED JUSTICE

A murder story inspired by true
events during the Wild West in Texas

Inspired by Actual Events

Christopher Molleda

RESTRAINED JUSTICE
A MURDER STORY INSPIRED BY TRUE EVENTS
DURING THE WILD WEST IN TEXAS

iUniverse books may be ordered through booksellers or by contacting:

iUniverse
1663 Liberty Drive
Bloomington, IN 47403
www.iuniverse.com
1-800-Authors (1-800-288-4677)

ISBN: 978-1-5320-8076-0 (sc)
ISBN: 978-1-5320-8075-3 (e)

Library of Congress Control Number: 2019912612

Print information available on the last page.

iUniverse rev. date: 08/26/2019

CONTENTS

Part I: Murder
and
Investigation

Part II: The Trial

INTRODUCTION

This is the tale of William Faust, the town druggist who was brought to answer for a heinous crime he may have committed in 1874. A family's child was murdered, and Mrs. Faust was nearly murdered in the same spree while she stayed with a family friend. Both Mrs. Faust and the child were bludgeoned by a man with an ax. The crime took place in New Braunfels, Texas, during the era of the Wild West just ten years after the American Civil War and the passing of the Thirteenth Amendment. Mr. Faust claimed he was innocent; and his wife, who was blind for life from the attack, believed her husband's innocence. While Faust was jailed awaiting trial, an even darker side began to emerge about William Faust's past, casting more suspicion on past unsolved murders. Meanwhile, a former slave, minding his own business, unknowingly became a key witness to the crime. The nation would test its resolve as a former Confederate state now needed to rely on this most valuable eyewitness to the violent crime. The town had to decide who they would believe: Faust's beloved wife, who was herself a victim, or a former slave? The locals were demanding justice over an innocent thirteen-year-old's slaying, creating a tremendous burden on a local sheriff, who had to uphold the law of the land by trying to bring a man in to face justice.

PART I

MURDER
AND
INVESTIGATION

CHAPTER 1

THE FAUSTS

July 5ᵗʰ 1874

Mr. William Faust, a stocky German man in his early forties, co-owned a pharmacy in downtown New Braunfels, Texas. Tonight he was starting the dreaded and overdue inventory. The pharmacy was in the middle of town in the square next to Mr. Faust's best customer, Dr. Rhein, a fifty-year-old German immigrant with a jolly personality.

Faust lived with his wife in the next town down the Guadalupe River in Seguin, Texas. The in- laws lived in the same town but communicated seldom after the marriage.

William Faust had just closed the pharmacy when Dr. Rhein knocked on the door.

Annoyed, Faust answered, and the doctor pushed in past him. William grumbled, "Yes, Doctor, what is the emergency?"

William was not usually rude, but he had closed the pharmacy to begin his inventory and was mildly irritated.

Dr. Rhein was a little hard of hearing and unintentionally spoke loudly, but he was always in a pleasant mood. He said, "I have a bit of a problem, William. My horse was sick, and I had to put it down. Can I use your horse to go to San Antonio? I have to put some money on a piece of land I purchased."

William knew that Dr. Rhein provided him plenty of customers and his practice being so close was an asset to him, so, relenting, he said, "I am sorry I came off a bit nasty. It's just this inventory I've got to get done. I guess I can let you use one of my horses. I am going to be here all night."

Dr. Rhein excitedly said, "Thank you, thank you. Of course, I will pay you and leave you a deposit in case anything happens."

He opened a large bag, pulled out a one hundred dollar bill, and handed it to Faust, who noticed a hefty amount of cash in the bag. William thought how easy it would be to take the cash and be rid of the doctor. He reminded himself that he would never do such a thing, but there were many who would not think twice. William's life of relative poverty was the genesis of such thoughts. William had courted Helen Rhodius and proposed to Helen, who was from a prosperous family, and that placed him on the right path.

William said, "Take Moose. He is watered and ready to go."

"Thank you, William. I will have him back right where he is now by tomorrow morning."

"No problem, and be careful."

• •

William finished up a few hours later, still not nearly having completed his inventory, and locked the pharmacy. He began his ride along the Guadalupe River to his home with his older horse that usually carried additional load back home. It was already dark, and he thought his wife would not be home; surprisingly, she was still there to collect things to stay with the Voelckers for a week in preparation for his long upcoming work nights. Helen, William's wife, usually stayed with the Voelkers because she was scared to be alone. A few months previously, some strange men came to her home looking for someone named Faust. The men scared Helen, and she had not been able to be in the home without William since. William assured her that they were looking for his brother, not him. Nevertheless, it created an annoying phobia.

William decided to go to bed and expected his wife to make breakfast in the morning. He was tired of coming home to an empty bed and no supper. William knew that Helen would only be home once a week while he conducted inventory. The next morning William was awakened just after sunrise by Helen and the aroma of breakfast.

He went downstairs and saw a plate of *wurst* (sausage) and bread rolls with eggs prepared for him.

Helen said, "Morning, my love. Are you going to be working late tonight?"

He said, "Yes, I have at least a week of inventory at the pharmacy; you know how this works."

Helen said, "Okay, I will stay with the Voelckers then. I hate it when you are not here for the night. Where is Moose?"

William was growing tired of her phobia. He took a bite of his breakfast and said, "Dr. Rhein borrowed him. He left me a deposit in case something happened to Moose."

Helen asked, "What happened to his horse?"

William took another bite and said, "I think the horse broke his leg, and he had to put it down."

Helen said, "My sister is coming back in a few weeks; she will be staying with my mom until she gets married."

William thought of Helen's sister, Elena, the younger, more beautiful of the sisters, and the one he originally wanted to marry. Of course, she would be getting a part of the family

3

inheritance when Helen's mother passed. He said, "Well, I guess that will be okay if she keeps your mom company."

Mrs. Faust looked at Mr. Faust and sternly said, "We live in a strong Catholic home and town. I am sure she will find someone like you to join our family soon."

William was annoyed. He paused, looked at his wife, and said, "As long as you start staying here more often. It's nice to have a meal waiting for me."

Mr. Faust thought of something that had happened to his cousin. His wife had died from smallpox, and he married again into the same family by marrying his wife's younger sister.

Helen said, "My mom knew I was well off with you, and my sis has not started her life. They want her to have a good life like me." Helen's father had passed a few years earlier.

William, with contempt in his voice, said, "Well, is she going to share that money with you?"

"I told my mom I was happy and my little sister did not have anyone to take care of her, so I refused any money."

Quickly standing from his breakfast, William said, "Well, thanks for thinking of us, I am leaving for town."

William was disgruntled. He hated working and wanted a life of servants. He knew that slavery was over and he would need a large amount of money to establish such a lifestyle. He had not anticipated working anymore when he discovered his in-laws were very wealthy, but now he understood that this was no longer possible as long as he was married to Helen.

. . . .

When William got back to town to open the pharmacy, he realized that his horse Moose was not there and Dr. Rhein's office was closed.

A patient was waiting out front; it was a woman who was

also William's customer. She asked Mr. Faust, "Have you seen Dr. Rhein? I had an 8:00 a.m. appointment."

William replied, "Well, I lent him my horse and I see it's not here yet, so he must be gone still."

William looked through the window of Dr. Rhein's office, and it appeared that he had not been there at all this morning. Dr. Rhein usually left a sign when he would return. Mr. Faust opened the door to his pharmacy and went inside.

William began his normal routine, but then he heard a frantic knock at the door. It was Mrs. Rhein.

Annoyed, William yelled, "I do not open for a few minutes still! Can I help you?"

Mrs. Rhein frantically said, "Yes, yes. My husband did not come home last night. I know he was going to borrow a horse to go into town."

William told her, "Yes, ma'am, it was me who lent him my horse, but he did not bring it back yet."

Mrs. Rhein asked, "Did you see him this morning?"

William said, "No, I did not see him. That is the strange thing about all this. My horse was not here this morning."

Mrs. Rhein said, "I need to go to the sheriff. In twenty-five years he has never done this. Something is wrong."

William said, "I am sure he is around here somewhere, ma'am."

Mrs. Rhein abruptly left, and William prepared to open the pharmacy.

Mr. Faust dealt with a few customers but mainly prepared for his month-end audit. He was once again interrupted when Sheriff Charles Saur, a tall, slender man with blond-whitish hair who had a rough cowboy face, and Deputy Schmidt, also a young man of German descent, entered the store. William looked up at the sheriff and said, "Hello, Sheriff and Deputy. Can I help you?"

Sheriff Saur asked, "Can we talk somewhere?"

William was expecting this and knew he had to keep his cool with the law. "Sure," he replied. "Let's talk in my office."

Sheriff Saur said, "Mrs. Rhein came in and said you were the last one to talk to her husband before he disappeared. Can you tell me what happened?"

William was uncomfortable with this conversation and replied, "Sheriff, I lent him my horse yesterday. He said his horse was injured, and he paid me to use one of mine. It was not here this morning."

Sheriff Saur asked, "Did you talk to him this morning?"

William thought he'd given a good answer and was suspicious of why the sheriff was so persistent with his questioning. He said, "No, my horse was not there. I borrowed one of Mr. Voelcker's horses. Is Mr. Rhein okay?"

The sheriff did not say anything but stared at William, who became uncomfortable when the sheriff did not say anything. The sheriff was a lifelong lawman and had dealt with many conflicts in the territory. There were bandits who rode in and out of the area, and he had tangled with the worst of the worst. The sheriff knew he did not have any evidence, but he did not like the fact that William was one of the last persons to see Dr. Rhein.

After a long pause, Sheriff Saur said, "We do not know right now. Did you know he had a large amount of cash with him?"

William said, "I can imagine he did. He said he was going to San Antonio to make a deposit into his bank or a land deal or something like that."

Sheriff Saur never stopped staring directly at Mr. Faust. He had years of intuition from being a lawman that had triggered his suspicions when he questioned Faust. He said, "I will be in touch if we need to talk to you; in the meantime, I am going to send a telegraph to the Bexar County folks to see if we have any reported holdups along the way. Good day, sir."

William sat back down, very uneasy with the way Sheriff Saur had talked to him. Mr. Faust continued his inventory for the next few days. He stayed an extra hour each day, extending his long days since he had to make up for the interruptions. Helen continued to sleep over at the Voelckers' home since she feared to stay without him in the house. Helen slept in the thirteen-year-old daughter's bed; her name was Emma Voelcker and she slept in the living room when Helen stayed. Helen's phobia seemed to be getting worse. William knew she was scared and knew she often slept in Emma's bed.

A stranger was spotted once again near the Voelckers' and Fausts' homes, which raised concerns again for William and the Voelckers. William planned to have a late drink in nearby Seguin with a friend at a saloon later that night to celebrate his progress on the inventory. William had friends in Seguin and stayed at a Stagecoach Inn there often, including a mistress who frequented the inn. He was simply growing tired of going to an empty home and getting tired of Helen. He would often sleep at the hotel and stop by his house just to check on things. William locked up and then rode his horse to Seguin.

CHAPTER 2

EMMA AND THE VOELCKER FAMILY

The Voelckers were a happy family that loved life and were willing to take on any challenge that came their way. The family emigrated from Germany in the mid-1800s to Texas. This was a time of conflict shortly after the Texas Revolution in the quest for independence. This was also a time when the United States was divided into the North and the South, and Texas was drawn into a bloody Civil War over slavery. Julius Voelcker soon found himself an officer in the nation's deadliest conflict ever. The Germans and Mexicans did not necessarily believe in slavery; however, the issue of war forced Texas residents to pick a side, and it was not wise to pick the North so deep in a state mostly loyal to the South.

After Julius married Louisa, the two started a family with a daughter and son, Emma and (three years later) Emil. They were said to have been influential in starting the town of New Braunfels, Texas. Julius lived his life as a farmer, and the family lived near the Guadalupe River. Life was simple for the family, and Julius invested in owning a pharmacy, entrusting William Faust to run it for him while he raised his family on the farm. Emil who was eleven years old and Emma were both hardworking and spirited children for their age. The Civil War was over, and financially the South suffered and the North prospered. Julius taught his family that in the United States, hard work led to prosperity and reward. The Voelckers were a strong, industrious family who relied on each other for success.

• •

July 18, 1874

Morning on the Voelcker farm started before sunrise. The entire family knew their duties. Julius tended to the fields for planting seasonal crops, Emma's routine was milking the cows, Emil had to feed the pigs, and Louisa supported the whole operation from inside the home, often helping Emma. Louisa served a quick breakfast, and the family was back at work. Dinner was served the last part of the day, and Louisa always prepared a good supper for the family after a hard July day in Texas.

Young Emma led the family in grace before the family ate. She closed her eyes, and the family held hands as Emma began her prayer. "Dear Lord, thank you for the food you have provided for us. May it be beneficial to our bodies and give us the strength to start a new day."

Julius said to Louisa, "I know we have an upcoming festival. How are the dance classes going?"

Emma anxiously said, "Pa, it's going good. I am really learning the dances, and I will be ready by October."

Louisa said, "She is doing great; in fact, I am proud of her."

Julius chewed his food and looked proudly at Emma. "It's amazing how fast you learn, This family is proud."

Emil said, "Dancing? I am too tired to do anything after working. Pa, maybe Emma should feed the pigs."

Julius looked at Emil and said, "I am sure Emma can do both."

Louisa said, "Okay, that is enough. Emma, as soon as you're done, wash up and get ready for your dance class. Mrs. Mueller will be here to pick you up in an hour."

Emma excused herself from the table and kissed her parents. She went to her room to begin washing up.

Louisa yelled, "Mrs. Faust will be sleeping in your bed when you get home, so you may have to sleep on the floor."

Emma said, "Okay, Momma." Emma loved Mrs. Faust, and Mrs. Faust loved Emma. Mrs. Faust wanted to have children like the Voelcker family.

CHAPTER 3

DR. RHEIN WAS FOUND MURDERED, LIKELY ROBBED MID JULY1874

William locked up, turned to his horse, and was startled by two men—Sheriff Saur and Deputy Schmidt. Sheriff Saur said, "Mr. Faust, we need to talk to you at the jail. We just got a telegram from Bexar County/ Dr. Rhein was found murdered just over the county line."

William looked stunned and said, "Sheriff, I have told you everything I know already. What is the meaning of this?"

Deputy Schmidt answered, "That is exactly why we are going to talk to you."

William followed the sheriff and Deputy Schmidt to the sheriff's office. The sheriff said, "Have a seat, Mr. Faust."

William sat down, and the sheriff began to ask questions. "Mr. Faust, can you tell me once again what exactly happened the last time you spoke with Dr. Rhein?"

William was frustrated and disgusted with having to answer questions once again, and he was irritated at being pulled away from his work at the pharmacy. He answered,

"Well, I told you the doctor asked to borrow my horse, which I guess is gone now. I did lend him my horse, and he told me that he was going to San Antonio to put some money down on a property. He gave me a $100 security deposit for the horse; I have not spoken to him since nor seen him."

Sheriff Saur asked, "Where did you go after the doctor left the pharmacy?"

William blurted out, "I was there doing inventory, closed the store, and then left to my house."

Deputy Schmidt said, "We have reason to believe that Dr. Rhein never left New Braunfels because he was supposed to pick up some documents from his home before he left for San Antonio."

William was quiet for a moment and finally said, "Well, I guess that is something you guys have to figure out. I do not know what else to tell you."

Deputy Schmidt asked, "Did you go anywhere near Bexar County in the past few days?"

William turned red and was quiet. He then said, "I told you I was here and at my home; that is it. Why do you ask?"

Deputy Schmidt leaned over closer to William and said, "The sheriff's posse in Bexar County has reports of a man matching your description selling a horse like the one you lent Dr. Rhein."

William was angry and said, "Well, that is obviously not me. Look, if you are going to arrest me, then arrest me; if not, I have work to do."

Sheriff Saur and Deputy Schmidt stared at William and did not say a word. After a moment, Sheriff Saur said, "We are done … for now."

William stormed out of the jail office, irritated at the whole ordeal and in disbelief at the way the sheriff was handling him.

Sheriff Saur said, "You know, there still is something about him that is not adding up."

Deputy Schmidt said, "I have a strong feeling he is behind this robbery and disappearance. Even though he married into a good family, I have my doubts about him."

The sheriff said, "Keep a close eye on him; I just don't like the feeling I get about him."

Deputy Schmidt said, "I plan on keeping two eyes on him."

CHAPTER 4

A NIGHT OF TERROR

July 22–23, 1874

The night was young in New Braunfels, Texas, and Mr. Faust worked late once again. He knew his wife would not stay at his house and would be at the Voelckers' home. That night, like all Thursday nights, Julius and Louisa Voelcker sent their daughter to a German folk dancing class, escorted by a nearby neighbor who picked her up and dropped her off. The Voelckers were asleep in an upstairs bedroom. Mrs. Faust was asleep in Emma Voelcker's bed, and the Voelckers' son was in the next room, both located downstairs.

It was 8:15 p.m. when Emma was escorted home by her neighbor. Emma got ready for bed by candlelight; it was a beautiful bright night due to a full moon. She knew she was supposed to sleep in the same room as Mrs. Faust, who was scared to be by herself. At nearly 10:45 p.m., Emma had fallen asleep; she was tired from the long dancing lessons but wished to perform at the upcoming German October celebration that took place in three months.

Emma was awakened at 1:00 a.m. by what she thought was the back door opening; she assured herself everything was fine and fell back asleep. Emma woke up again and heard footsteps; she looked over to Mrs. Faust, who was fast asleep. Emma looked to the other side, and a man was standing with an ax raised above his head, already in motion striking down toward her head. She was instantly mortally wounded. The blow was so vicious her head was split from the forehead down to her ears.

Mrs. Faust was instantly awakened and screamed, but a brutal swing of the ax struck her forehead and knocked her out cold. The man with the ax quickly walked out of the room, turned, and saw the young Voelcker son looking at him in the dark of the night. Emil yelled in German, "Get out, get out!" The man purposely turned his face away and tilted his hat to hide his face; the young man ran to the door and saw a dark figure fleeing on horseback at full gallop.

The boy screamed, "*Mom, Mom!*"

Louisa and Julius ran down the stairs and saw their son terrified with fright at the bottom of the stairs.

Julius grabbed his son and said, "What is going on?"

He pointed to Emma's room, crying hysterically. Julius looked toward the room, walked into it, and said, "Lord Jesus."

Louisa attempted to run into the room, but Julius grabbed her and said, "Do not go in there. Take our son to the neighbors. I have got to get the sheriff."

Julius checked his daughter and Mrs. Faust. He knew they were dead or near dead, and he needed to get his family to safety. Grabbing his rifle, he saddled his horse to escort his frightened family to nearby neighbors.

Louisa screamed, "My baby, we cannot leave my baby!"

Julius said, "Honey, go with Emil. I will try to save her. Get to safety."

Louisa continued to scream. "*No, no!*"

15

Julius had to grab her and pull her on the horse, giving his rifle to his son to hold.

Julius yelled as he rode past homes, "Murder, murder, there has been a murder in my home!"

Neighbors began to wake, and a town woke to assist and help their fellow citizens in distress.

The Voelckers arrived at the closest neighbors' house, and Julius knocked on the door.

Mr. Schaefer said, "Julius, what is going on?"

Julius answered, "They killed my daughter and Mrs. Faust; can you watch my son and wife? I have got to get the sheriff."

Mr. Schaefer said, "Ma, help me and Julius come inside. I will go with you."

Julius said, "No, protect my family. I will be back with the sheriff."

Julius rode hard in the dark of the night. The sheriff lived only four miles from his home, but it seemed like a hundred miles. Julius arrived at the sheriff's home, heard dogs barking, and noticed that his horse was breathing hard. Julius frantically knocked and knocked and yelled, "Sheriff, it is Julius. I need your help."

Julius heard movement and saw a candle being lit in a bedroom.

The sheriff came out and yelled, "What in the hell happened, Julius?"

Hunched over, Julius said, "I need you to come to my house; Mrs. Faust and my daughter have been murdered."

The sheriff said, "Dear Lord, I will get my horse ready. Who did this?"

Julius was still hunched over and tearfully said, "I do not know; I could not even tell who my daughter was or Mrs. Faust, there is so much blood in my daughter's room."

The sheriff came out from the back with his horse and asked, "Julius, where is the rest of your family?"

Julius said, "I took them to the Schaefers, the closest home to my house."

The sheriff said, "Okay, let's ride. You lead the way."

The two rode hard through the night, both of their horses at a full gallop through the windy countryside. They finally stopped at the house, both horses breathing heavily. The sheriff drew his sidearm and went into the house, with Julius following close behind.

The sheriff said, "Julius, wait here, and I will check things out. Light some candles so we can see in here."

Julius lit a candle and handed it to the sheriff, who walked into Emma's room. He bent down, took off his hat, and said, "Mother of God, who could do such a thing?"

Julius said, "I do not know. My daughter is innocent; I think they were after Mrs. Faust."

The sheriff checked Emma and did not see her breathing. He then checked Mrs. Faust and saw her chest move. He bent further to listen for a breath.

The sheriff yelled, "Quickly, grab some more blankets; she is still breathing. We need to take her to a doctor."

Julius looked at Mrs. Faust and asked, "Is my daughter alive?"

The sheriff said, "No, I'm sorry, Julius. If we can save Mrs. Faust, we may find out who did this."

The sheriff and Julius bandaged Mrs. Faust as best they could and loaded her up on the sheriff's horse; he knew Dr. Rhein was missing, so he had to ride farther, to Dr. Lehde's house.

The sheriff said, "Guard the house, and I will send for my posse to help you here."

The sheriff rode off at a full gallop in the dead of the night.

Mr. Voelcker knew he had to face the brutal fact that his daughter was dead. He could not think of anyone who would want to hurt his daughter and thought of the fear Mrs. Faust had had the past few weeks.

The sheriff stopped two miles away from the Voelckers at Deputy Schmidt's house.

The sheriff whistled loudly near Deputy Schmidt's home, fired a shot in the air, and loudly called out, "Murder, murder at the Voelckers' home!" Deputy Schmidt knew the routine and immediately recognized that it was the sheriff summoning him.

Deputy Schmidt came out and asked, "Yes, Sheriff, what happened, and who is that?"

The sheriff said, "This is Mrs. Faust; she is barely alive. I am going to Dr. Lehde's, and I need you to stop by Deputy Schultz's and head to the Voelckers. Emma was murdered."

Deputy Schmidt said, "Oh my God, I will saddle up and head down there."

The sheriff said, "I will be back as soon as I can. In the meantime, hold the scene down; nobody goes in or out. Ask the usual questions."

Deputy Schmidt said, "I will be there in thirty minutes."

The sheriff quickly rode off. He cast a wary eye at Mrs. Faust, who was still losing a lot of blood from her head.

The sheriff said, "Hang in there. The doc is going to stitch you up."

The sheriff arrived at the doctor's home, carried Mrs. Faust over his shoulder, and banged on the door. He finally heard movement inside the home, and Dr. Lehde asked, "Who is it? Sheriff, is that you?"

The sheriff yelled, "It's me! Open up, Doc. She is not doing too good."

The doctor asked, "What happened? Lay her on the table."

The doctor looked at her and said, "She has lost a lot of blood. Sheriff, get my bag; it is right behind you."

The doctor removed the wrap from Mrs. Faust's head and saw a large gash above her eyes. He began to clean the wound and sew it shut. The doctor said, "It looks like she was hit with an ax."

The sheriff said, "I think so too, Doc. Young little Emma's head was split open down from her forehead to her ears, and she isn't alive." He then added, "I need to get back to the Voelckers' house. Do what you can."

The sheriff made his way back to the Voelckers' home, the sun would rise in a few hours, and he needed to see what evidence was available. He found his deputies were at the Voelckers, and he met with them in front of the house.

Deputy Schmidt asked, "Sheriff, is Mrs. Faust going to make it?"

The sheriff replied, "She does not look good; she has lost a lot of blood."

Deputy Schmidt nodded his head and said, "Sheriff, we have looked around the place. We did not find a bloody stick or knife on the property, and I do not believe any family had anything to do with this."

The sheriff said, "We need to find Mr. Faust and let him know what has happened to his wife. Deputy Wilkins, ride to the Faust house at first light and let him know where his wife is and what happened."

Deputy Schmidt asked, "Sheriff, did you ride north out of here?"

Sheriff Saur said, "Those are my tracks. I rode north."

Deputy Schmidt said, "I found some tracks that go south toward the Guadalupe River."

The sheriff said, "Let's track the trail and see where it goes.

19

Mr. Voelcker, we found a trail, and we are going to follow it. We will send the funeral parlor and church folks to you."

Mr. Voelcker said, "Thank you, Sheriff. Get whoever did this to my daughter."

The sheriff and Deputy Schmidt followed the trail that hugged the Guadalupe River. They traveled steadily along the narrow path until they could no longer track the route. The tracks ended south toward Seguin. A sense of fear and of duty awakened the city of New Braunfels as nearly twenty riders were gathered within a half hour and rode out to search for suspects and warn nearby towns.

CHAPTER 5

THE BURIAL: A UNIFIED TOWN SAYS GOODBYE TO AN ANGEL

The sheriff went to his office downtown; he sent his deputies to pick up any stranger or anyone suspicious around town. He waited for Mr. Faust so he could tell him personally that his wife was likely not alive. The sheriff had never seen a child so brutally murdered; he knew the news of the murder would spread quickly, and the peaceful town would demand justice.

The sheriff had to think about his next move. He hoped that a deputy would have a suspect to bring in to answer for the crime. The town would be frightened if such a crime were not solved. The sheriff then heard the bell above the office door; it was the editor of the local newspaper.

Shawn Fitzgerald asked, "Sheriff, I hear we have a horrible crime that took place. What do you want in the papers?"

The sheriff asked, "How did you hear about this?"

Mr. Fitzgerald said, "I was at the church this morning; I saw your deputy and the priest leave in a hurry."

Sheriff Saur said, "We have had a horrible murder at the Voelckers' home. Helen Faust is likely dead also."

Mr. Fitzgerald looked concerned. "Two people murdered! Any suspects?"

Sheriff Saur replied, "That is all I have right now. These happened only hours ago. If you will excuse me, I have a lot to do."

Mr. Fitzgerald said, "I understand, Sheriff; you will keep me posted on the investigation?"

The sheriff nodded. "The town will know when we have something. For now we have to honor the deceased and prepare for a burial."

Deputy Schultz and Deputy Wilkins walked in with three men. Deputy Schultz said, "We have picked up these three around town; they are strangers."

Sheriff Saur said, "We will question them when they sober up. I do not see blood on their clothes, and I am going to tell Mr. Faust the bad news."

Sheriff Saur did not see anyone at Mr. Faust's pharmacy, so he rode to the home miles from town toward Seguin. Upon arrival at the home, he knocked on the door. There was no answer, only silence. Sheriff Saur rounded the house looking through the windows, but there was no sign of anyone inside. The sheriff checked for their horses and noticed that one of the horses and a saddle was missing.

Sheriff Saur did not know what to think of Mr. Faust's disappearance, but one way or another, he needed to find Mr. Faust, who might have answers for the mysterious murders. The sheriff went back into town to his office. For now, he would shut down and prepare for the burial of the dead. He next went to Dr. Lehde's office to check on Mrs. Faust.

Sheriff Saur went into the doctor's office and saw Dr. Lehde. Mrs. Faust was bandaged up, lying on a bed in the doctor's office. Dr. Lehde motioned for him to be quiet, and the two stepped into his office.

Sheriff Saur asked, "How is she, Doctor?"

Dr. Lehde said, "Sheriff, she is not doing so well. I do not expect her to make it through the week, but she is alive now and needs rest."

Sheriff Saur asked, "Has Mr. Faust been told the news by anyone? I cannot find him and am not sure he knows of this."

Dr. Lehde said, "I know William. I am surprised he is not at his pharmacy. I usually see him daily."

Sheriff Saur said, "If he comes here before I find him, can you let me know? He may be the only one who has any answers for what happened last night."

Dr. Lehde replied, "I sure will, Sheriff."

Sheriff Saur went to his office, and Deputy Schultz was waiting for him.

Deputy Schultz said, "We have nothing, Sheriff. The church is going to help prepare Emma for burial and help the family."

Sheriff Saur took off his hat, sat on his chair, and said, "Nothing like this should happen to such a beautiful family or any family. Go send word to Detective Lyons that we need him on this case after the family and the town grieve for this angel whom we lost."

Deputy Schultz said, "Right away, sir. I will stop by and notify Detective Lyons. I think he will be at the courthouse. See you tomorrow, Sheriff. They want to bury her right away."

Sheriff Saur said, "Thank you, and put the word out we need to find Mr. Faust."

As Deputy Schultz walked out, a man handed him a telegram. Deputy Schultz said, "Sheriff, it is for you, from Austin."

The sheriff read the telegram and said, "Damn, it's from

Governor Coke. Word spreads fast. He is offering a five-hundred-dollar reward for the apprehension of the murderer." The sheriff also had received word that the city council approved an additional five-hundred-dollar award and authorization for a twelve-man posse to guard the city and round up suspects.

July 24, 1874

• •

    The funeral service was incredibly somber. Emma Voelcker was depicted as the precious daughter that her parents loved. The priest said that "justice is in the eye of the beholder."

    A band played "Amazing Grace," and the funeral procession was the largest in the county's history as everyone who could come to the funeral had made their way there. The procession was over half a mile long, with folks in carriages, on horseback, and on foot. The Voelcker family was devastated, and the priest said his final blessing as Emma was laid to rest in a closed casket. The family was greeted in line by the entire town. The sheriff was there, and he approached Mr. and Mrs. Voelcker and their ten-year-old son.

    The sheriff took off his hat and said, "Mr. and Mrs. Voelcker, I am deeply sorry for your loss, I just can't imagine how you feel."

    Mrs. Voelcker responded and said, "Sheriff, find this person and make him answer for what they did to my precious baby."

    The sheriff then went to Mr. Voelcker and extended his hand. Before he could say his condolences, Mr. Voelcker held the sheriff's hand and stared at him, saying, "Sheriff, before Faust disappeared, I asked him what happened. He did not seem sad but oddly worried about himself. He told me he could not talk about the murder since you made him uncomfortable about the doctor's disappearance. I asked him why he could not talk to you, and he said because he was worried about his wife. I just don't buy it; a father just knows. I trusted him at one time, but I do not anymore."

Sheriff Saur said, "I promise we will have every one of my men working on this case." The sheriff tipped his hat, then placed it back on his head, and again tipped it toward the family as a sign of respect.

CHAPTER 6

THE INVESTIGATION BEGINS

The sheriff left the following morning for his office. He had not slept much since the murder. He had seen plenty of blood and guts before, but nothing disturbed him as much as seeing the body of a child bludgeoned to death. He knew the vivid picture of the crime scene would never leave his mind. The sheriff opened the door to the office and saw that the three men in the holding cell had sobered up. Deputy Wilkins had pulled night duty and was ending his watch when he saw his boss.

The sheriff looked at the three men in the jail cell and asked Deputy Wilkins, "Did their stories check out?"

Deputy Wilkins said, "Yes, Sheriff, they're just transient drunks from San Antone. They did not have anything to do with the murder."

The sheriff said, "Let them out and give them their property back, then get some sleep. We will be working this all week or as long as it takes."

Deputy Schmidt and Detective Lyons walked in at the same time that Deputy Wilkins left. Deputy Schmidt said, "Morning, Sheriff. I take it we do not have much to go on."

The sheriff responded, "No, I just wish we knew what happened to Mr. Faust. I have had an uneasy feeling about him with the disappearance of Dr. Rhein."

Deputy Schmidt said, "Well, where do you want to start, Sheriff?"

The sheriff said, "Grab your things. We need to find something out about Mr. Faust's whereabouts. Lyons, we will fill you in on the way to the Faust house."

As the sheriff and Deputy Schmidt grabbed their gear, the door to the office suddenly opened. It was Mr. Faust.

The sheriff, Detective Lyons, and Deputy Schmidt all stared at Mr. Faust, and the sheriff broke the silence. "Mr. Faust, are you okay? I am not sure if you have been told. I have some bad news to tell you."

Mr. Faust said, "I know, Sheriff; I was in Seguin and came over here when I found out the news."

The sheriff looked at Deputy Schmidt but did not say anything.

Mr. Faust continued, "I have to thank you, Sheriff. Dr. Fitzgerald told me what happened. He said you took my wife to him."

The sheriff said, "I have been occupied with this investigation and the funeral. Do you have any news on how your wife is doing?"

Mr. Faust took his hat off, looked down, and spoke quietly. "The doctor does not think she is going to make it through the week. He says that I should prepare myself for the worst. Do you have any idea who did this, Sheriff?"

The sheriff said, "No, I do not. I was hoping you could shed some light on all this. We do not have much to go on. I do have to ask you where you have been and will you be assisting us in the hunt for this murderer?"

Mr. Faust looked up and said, "No, I do not know why

someone would do this. Maybe the Voelckers know something. I am afraid I won't be much help; my wife needs me. I would be distracted on her well-being and want to be at her side if she passes; I do not want her to be alone. Sheriff, I was in Seguin that night, and it got late, so I stayed at the Stagecoach Inn."

The sheriff looked at Mr. Faust the same way he did when he questioned him about Dr. Rhein's disappearance. He wanted to sit him down and interrogate him but knew it would be wrong if he was mistaken in any way. Nonetheless, the sheriff believed a man's instinct should be not to do nothing he should hunt the murderers down and take them to justice, dead or alive.

The sheriff said, "I want you to spend time with your wife and let us know if you have any idea who could do such a thing or may be capable of such an act."

Mr. Faust said, "No, I do not have any idea; this makes no sense to me."

The sheriff said, "When the time is right, we need to sit down and talk. We have no leads, so anything may help."

Mr. Faust said, "I will be in tomorrow as long as my wife does not take a turn for the worse."

Mr. Faust left the office, and the sheriff turned to Deputy Schmidt and Detective Lyons.

"Deputy Schmidt, keep an eye on Mr. Faust; and Detective Lyons, go to Seguin and establish Mr. Faust's whereabouts on that night and if he stayed at the Stagecoach Inn. Detective, we do not have much to go on except the fact that two people are likely murdered, Dr. Lehde thinks it was an ax, and we had a fresh trail we followed south from the home to the Guadalupe River before we lost the trail halfway to Seguin.

Deputy Schmidt and Detective Lyons both immediately left to commence their tasks.

Detective Lyons carefully rode the trail nearly four miles to Seguin on a pathway that curved along the Guadalupe River. He kept an eye out for anything that may have been left by the murderer. He did not see anything, and very likely the murder weapon had been tossed in the river. He did not notice anything except a black male fishing on a bank. Detective Lyons finally reached the town of Seguin, and a few miles in, he located the Stagecoach Inn. The inn was used as a stagecoach stop for people passing through the area. The inn had a small saloon for patrons and local prostitutes.

Detective Lyons stopped, entered the hotel, and met with the innkeeper.

Detective Lyons said, "Good day, sir. My name is Detective Lyons from Comal County. Do you have a moment and a place where we can talk?"

The innkeeper said, "My name is Roland Johnston. I am the owner of the inn. Let's talk in my office."

Detective Lyons said, "Why, thank you. What I am going to ask you about is an ongoing investigation. I am sure by now you have heard about the murders we had two days ago."

Mr. Johnson said, "Of course. What a tragedy."

Detective Lyons asked, "I would like you to keep this conversation confidential."

Mr. Johnston said, "No problem. What can I do for you?"

"I need to know if a Mr. Faust recently stayed here."

Mr. Johnston answered, "He did. I registered him. Let me look at the guest register."

Mr. Johnston showed the register to Detective Lyons and said, "It's right here. He signed in about 8:30 p.m. the night before the murder."

Detective Lyons asked, "Was there anything unusual about him, and did he leave and go anywhere?"

Mr. Johnston said, "He was my last guest that night; I

29

would not know if he left and not sure where he would have gone to if he did. Do you suspect him?"

Detective Lyons responded, "As of now, he seems to be a person of interest; we have to start somewhere. Thank you for your time, Mr. Johnston."

Detective Lyons had heard what he needed to clear Faust from being a suspect, but there still was the fact that he was not asleep at his own house in New Braunfels that needed some corroboration and elaboration. He rode back to New Braunfels and saw the same man fishing at the river, finishing up. They looked at each other, and Detective Lyons continued to New Braunfels. He walked into the sheriff's office and saw that the sheriff was being questioned by the editor of the newspaper. Detective Lyons could see the sheriff's patience wearing thin.

The sheriff saw Detective Lyons and said to the editor, "I have to talk to Detective Lyons in confidence now if you will leave so we can talk."

The editor left, and the sheriff turned to Detective Lyons. "What did you find out?"

Detective Lyons reported, "His story checks out. He was at the inn by 8:30 p.m., and nobody saw him leave the place."

The sheriff was quiet for a minute and then said, "Something just does not make sense. There is no motive for this murder, and there always is a motive."

Detective Lyons said, "I am going to the Voelckers' home and see if there is anything else we may find out."

Detective Lyons rode to the Voelckers' home and met with Mr. Voelcker. He took off his hat and again gave his condolences.

"I am sorry for your loss, but we need to discuss what happened so we can bring this man to justice."

Mr. Voelcker said, "Come on in; have a seat at the table."

Detective Lyons asked, "Can you tell me what you know about the night of the murder?"

Mr. Voelcker said, "There is not much we know. My wife and I were awoken by screams, and I found my daughter butchered and Mrs. Faust in bad shape."

Mr. Voelcker paused and said, "My son saw the man, but he is devastated. I think he is in shock."

Detective Lyons asked, "I really need to talk to him. It is important because the more time passes, the more people forget."

Mr. Voelcker called his son down, and Emil went to the table.

Detective Lyons said, "I am a deputy detective assigned to find your sister's killer. Can you tell me what happened?"

The younger brother did not look at Detective Lyons and did not say anything. Detective Lyons looked at Mr. Voelcker and said, "Can he talk? Is he okay?"

Mr. Voelcker spoke to his son in German. "Son, this man needs to know so he can solve this case. The killer can do this to someone else; it is okay to talk to him."

Emil spoke slowly and said, "I was woken up by terrible screams, I went to the hallway and saw a man, and he saw me. He was calm. He was holding an ax and wearing a coat and a hat. It was dark, but he hid his face by tucking his hat down and chin in his chest so I would not see his face. I yelled at him in German to get out, and he left on horseback at a full gallop."

Detective Lyons said, "Emil, you are a very brave boy. Did he look like anyone you have seen before?"

The boy said, "It was too dark. He was not a large man, but he was bigger than me."

Detective Lyons said, "Well, thank you again, and I am sorry for your loss. Let me assure you that I will not stop and the sheriff will not stop until we find out who and why they killed Emma."

Mr. Voelcker shed a visible tear and said, "Thank you very much, Detective."

Detective Lyons went back to report his findings to the sheriff at the office. The sheriff leaned back in his chair staring at the ceiling in deep thought.

Detective Lyons said, "Sheriff, I do not want to tell you we have a lot, but this is going to be like putting a puzzle together. Emil Voelcker got a glimpse of the murderer but could not recognize him."

Sheriff Saur said, "Well, shit, that is not much; we are back at square one."

Detective Lyons said, "No, Sheriff, it tells us a lot. The son described him as an average-size white male carrying an ax. He also said something very interesting; the man tucked his face away so Emil would not recognize him. I think that the suspect knows the family."

The sheriff said, "The Voelckers said they have not crossed paths with anyone they could think of."

Detective Lyons said, "I believe that. The Voelckers are a peaceful family. How is Mrs. Faust doing?"

Sheriff Saur said, "I do not think she is going to make it, and she may hold the answers to everything."

Detective Lyons said, "I will keep looking for answers, Sheriff. I do hate to admit this so early, but we are stuck until somebody comes forward or Mrs. Faust can tell us what happened."

Sheriff Saur said, "I know, and the governor and the town are going to want justice and answers. Let's post the five-hundred-dollar reward and see if anyone comes forward. We need to observe any deviation on how people act and make our next move, especially Faust."

Detective Lyons said, "I agree. Even criminals have codes they do not break; killing a child would be low even for the criminal world to accept."

Detective Lyons and Sheriff Saur were preparing to leave when they noticed Mr. and Mrs. Voelcker waving them down to talk to the lawmen.

Julius said, "I need to tell you something. My wife and I have had conversations with Mr. Faust. I spoke to him in private, and he said he would not talk about the murder or his injured wife. He has been very distant and not acting right; he won't let anyone talk to her."

Detective Lyons asked, "What do you mean not acting right?"

Julius responded, "Well, my neighbors are banding together to look for the suspect who murdered my precious girl and who caused harm to his wife. He is staying away from all of this. I think a normal man should be angry and go after the person who did this. He is not in any way interested; he is more concerned about her living than dying."

Louisa said, "I also pulled him to the side and asked him about the murder. He acted as if I was the law asking him, and he refused to answer any questions about the case. I was angry with him, and I said one final thing that made him uncomfortable. I told him that the murderer seemed to have knowledge of the layout of the house and had been there before. He froze and raised his voice, telling me that he was taking his wife back to his house. I tell you, this is not normal for a man who nearly lost his wife."

Sheriff Saur looked at Louisa and said, "Do you feel as a mother that the man who took your child's life could be William?"

Louisa looked up and said, "I know it is. I think you should go talk to Mrs. Rhodius, his mother-in-law."

Sheriff Saur said, "I will ride out there, I believe they live down by Cibolo Creek?"

Louisa confirmed, "Yes, they do."

Sheriff Saur looked to Detective Lyons and said, "Let's ride out that way."

• •

After about a forty-five-minute ride, Sheriff Saur and Detective Lyons arrived at the Rhodius ranch along Cibolo Creek. Mrs. Rhodius and her eldest son, Edward, were home. Sheriff Saur did not have any clue what to expect from the Rhodius family.

Sheriff Saur and Detective Lyons both took off their hats, and Sheriff Saur said, "Mrs. Rhodius, I know this is a hard time for you, and we are praying for your daughter's recovery."

Mrs. Rhodius said, "Sheriff, I would like you and your officer to come inside."

Detective Lyons and Sheriff Saur looked at each other and went inside the home.

Mrs. Rhodius seemed like a straightforward lady, and clearly there was an anger that would not let her be sad about her daughter. She felt that there would be plenty of time later to mourn and her daughter was hurt and still alive.

Mrs. Rhodius was direct and said, "Well, I am guessing you are here to talk to me about that no-good sonbitch William."

Sheriff Saur said, "Well, obviously you are not too fond of your son-in-law. What do you know?"

Mrs. Rhodius said, "Well, you know we are well off because we are hardworking, and William is not; he is a lazy son of a bitch."

Sheriff Saur said, "Do you think he would kill your daughter?"

Mrs. Rhodius said, "Yes. He wants to marry my youngest daughter. He has had his eye on her for a while, wants the rest of the money from our business."

Sheriff Saur asked, "Has William ever hurt your daughter?"

Mrs. Rhodius nodded and said, "Not physically, but I think he has tried to poison her. She is always sick and never used to be like that."

Sheriff Saur said, "Well, we will be looking at him very closely."

Mrs. Rhodius said, "I don't want him here; he may be fixing to leave, Sheriff."

She then added, "He asked Edward, my eldest son, for some money, and he did not feel safe. I told him not to give William any."

Sheriff Saur said, "I will be looking everywhere to find this killer, and if it turns out to be William, he will answer for this."

Mrs. Rhodius said, "Well, you should shoot the sonbitch. I know he did it."

The sheriff and Detective Lyons both thanked Mrs. Rhodius and left back to New Braunfels.

CHAPTER 7

A BREAK IN THE CASE

August 18, 1874

Nearly four weeks had gone by since the sinister murders, and there was no new evidence presented. The sheriff was under pressure from the mayor and even the governor of Texas to make an arrest. The sheriff thought that five hundred dollars would persuade friends or even relatives to turn each other in the name of justice. The sheriff called in Detective Lyons to go over what they had and approach the case from a different angle.

Detective Lyons said, "Morning, Sheriff. I guess nothing new on the Voelcker murder?"

Sheriff Saur said, "Nope, nothing at all. Let's go over this case and start fresh."

Detective Lyons said, "Mrs. Faust is still alive and at her house now. Mr. Faust and her sister are taking care of her."

Sheriff Saur said, "We need to go there today and check on her. If she has made it this long, I think she may pull through."

Detective Lyons said, "I know we are both thinking the same thing: something just does not add up with Mr. Faust's involvement."

The sheriff said, "I know. His alibi seems too good, but we have nothing to go on him."

Detective Lyons said, "Well, let's go to the Faust home and see if he changes his story."

The sheriff and Detective Lyons went to visit Mr. and Mrs. Faust at their home a few miles away. Mr. Faust was on the porch when the sheriff arrived.

The sheriff and Detective Lyons walked over to greet Mr. Faust. The sheriff said, "Morning, Mr. Faust. How is your wife?"

Mr. Faust paused and said, "She is doing okay. She actually spoke yesterday."

The two lawmen looked at each other, and Detective Lyons asked, "Did she say anything, and why did you not inform us?"

Mr. Faust responded, "She did not say anything, and I really cannot leave her alone; she can't see."

The sheriff asked, "Well, can we see her?"

Mr. Faust replied, "She is still not feeling up to seeing anyone."

Detective Lyons said, "Mr. Faust, we have no leads on the person who murdered Emma. Anything may help."

Mr. Faust looked down and said, "All right. Come on in."

The sheriff said, "We will have Detective Lyons go in, and we can stay out here and talk, Mr. Faust."

Detective Lyons walked in and saw Mrs. Faust lying in bed. She was bandaged all over the top of her head, including her eyes.

Detective Lyons said, "Mrs. Faust, I am Detective Lyons. Can you hear me?"

Detective Lyons asked again, "Mrs. Faust, can you hear me?"

Mrs. Faust did not say anything, and the detective made his way to the door. Then he heard a weak voice say, "Yes."

"Mrs. Faust, can you answer a few questions?"

After a pause, Mrs. Faust said, "Yes."

Detective Lyons spoke slowly. "Do you know who did this to you?"

Mrs. Faust said, "No … I woke up and was hit … The last thing I remember was waking up … not being able to see … did not see who did it."

Detective Lyons said, "I will be checking on you every week, and I am trying to find who did this."

The detective walked out of the home and noticed that the sheriff was on his horse ready to go. Detective Lyons also got on his horse and said to Mr. Faust, "Good day. We will be in touch."

The sheriff told Detective Lyons when they were away from the house, "He is still sticking to his story. Did she say anything?"

Detective Lyons nodded. "She was barely able to speak but said that she woke up and was struck. The last thing she remembered was waking up weeks later and not being able to see."

The sheriff said, "It seems like we are right back where we started. I am starting to think a drifter who is long gone may have done this."

Detective Lyons said, "Sheriff, I think he is still here."

• •

It was now October 4, 1874, and still there was no arrest. The sheriff and Detective Lyons returned to their office from a day of court on unrelated crimes. They both noticed a black man waiting for them at the sheriff's office, the same person Detective Lyons saw fishing on the Guadalupe River.

The gentleman said, "Sir, sorry to bother you. My name

is Isom Taylor. I was a slave ten years ago, but I work where I can find it."

Isom Taylor was a large black man and former slave who was now free after the Union victory in the American Civil War. He had large, workingman's hands, and a gentle, slow, submissive voice. He worked hard all his life and had a tough time living in the South finding work. There were many times he was paid very little or not at all. The law did not intervene in his favor, and he struggled like many former slaves finding a living.

The sheriff asked, "What exactly can I do for you?"

Mr. Taylor looked down and said, "Well, I am scared to tell you, but I know it is the right thing to do. The night of the murder of young Emma, I was fishing on the Guadalupe for some catfish. I saw a man on horseback, and things just did not look right."

Detective Lyons's interest was now piqued. "Did you recognize the man?"

Mr. Taylor looked down and said, "Yes, I did … it was Mr. Faust."

Detective Lyons asked, "What time would you say it was?"

Mr. Taylor said, "It was probably about one forty-five in the morning, about when the moon went down."

Sheriff Saur said, "I admire your courage telling us this. In a perfect world, this would be enough, but we have some people who are still sore over the war that would not recognize you as an equal."

Mr. Taylor replied, "I know, sir, but that girl did not deserve to die. Whether I will be believed or not, it is the right thing to do to tell what I saw no matter who I am. I do not care what people think of me; I was afraid no one would believe me if I reported this."

Detective Lyons continued, "So, tell us how you knew it was Mr. Faust and what exactly happened that night."

Mr. Taylor explained, "I heard a horse coming on the trail and saw a man coming. He had a large stick or maybe an ax, and he just threw it in the water. I finished my fishing and rode back on my horse to town, and he saw me. I glanced at him, and when I did, he tucked his hat down and his chin so I would not see him. I remember Mr. Faust from the Voelcker's Pharmacy where he worked. He made me order from the back of the store. I understand why, but it brought me face-to-face with him."

Sheriff Saur looked at Mr. Taylor and then at Detective Lyons and said, "I believe him. What do you think?"

Detective Lyons said, "I believe him, but is the judge going to sign a warrant for Mr. Faust's arrest?"

Sheriff Saur said, "You let me take care of that. We need to find that ax so it backs up the story. Have Mr. Taylor show you where this spot is, and take Deputy Schultz with you. And Mr. Taylor, do not tell anyone about this until we figure out how we are going to deal with it."

Mr. Taylor said, "I won't say anything, sir. I had trouble telling you all."

Detective Lyons, Deputy Schultz, and Mr. Taylor went to the Guadalupe River to find the ax. The sheriff went to discuss the warrant with the judge.

• •

The three lawmen went nearly halfway to Seguin along the Guadalupe and found the spot.

Deputy Schultz said, "If you can swim, take off your boots and let's find the ax."

Detective Lyons and Mr. Taylor began the long process

of diving and feeling for an ax; the water was not deep in the part they were searching. The three looked for nearly an hour, and there was no sign of an ax.

Detective Lyons asked, "Are you sure it is this spot?"

Mr. Taylor said, "I am positive. This is the spot I fish in. I can find this spot at daytime or night; that oak tree that grows sideways across the bank is the mark."

Detective Lyons griped, "Shit, I have not found anything." He started to walk back in the waist-high water, but then … "Wait a minute. I just knocked over something." He dove in the water and came up with an ax!

Detective Lyons looked at the ax and said, "Will you look at that? It looks like the initials WF etched into it."

Deputy Schultz said, "Let's get back and arrest this son of a bitch."

. . . .

Sheriff Saur knocked on the door of the judge's office, and Judge Rommel said, "Come on in."

Sheriff Saur said, "Afternoon, Judge. Do you have a moment?"

The judge replied, "I hope this is something about the Voelcker case."

Sheriff Saur said, "Actually, I do have something."

The judge took his glasses off and excitedly said, "Come on in. What do you have?"

Sheriff Saur said, "I have a witness who saw Mr. Faust going to Seguin after one forty-five, right after the murders took place; he lied to us."

The judge asked, "Who told you this?"

Sheriff Saur said, "It was a Negro man named Isom Taylor."

The judge said, "You want me to take a sworn statement from a former slave and have an innocent man, until proven guilty, go to jail and have him answer for a murder while his wife is on her deathbed? Why has he not finished the job? He has had plenty of opportunity."

Sheriff Saur said, "I believe him, and he also said he saw him with the murder weapon, an ax."

The judge said, "Have you found this murder weapon, and do you believe this man?"

Sheriff Saur said, "I believe this man, but I do not have the murder weapon. My posse is searching for it as we speak."

The judge said, "If you find the murder weapon, I will sign an arrest warrant but not without it."

Sheriff Saur offered, "If we do not find it, I will swear to the statement myself."

The judge said, "I know you are under a lot of pressure to have an arrest, but no, I will not."

Sheriff Saur countered, "Yes, I am under a lot of pressure, but I know you will be also if you know you have a witness who names Mr. Faust as a suspect. The town will be outraged."

The judge snapped back, "I will do what is right in the interest of justice. We cannot just make an arrest for something as serious as murder and have the case thrown out."

The judge and Sheriff Saur heard a lot of commotion coming up the stairs, and the door to the judge's office swung open. It was Detective Lyons and Deputy Schultz, still soaked from the swim in the river.

Detective Lyons said, "Excuse us, Sheriff and Your Honor, for the interruption; we have the ax with what looks like Mr. Faust's initials."

The judge and the sheriff smiled, and the judge said, "Draft the warrant. I will sign it."

CHAPTER 8

THE SEARCH FOR FAUST

The sheriff had the judge sign the arrest warrant, and it was ordered confidential until it was executed. The sheriff walked back into his office, where Deputy Schultz, Deputy Schmidt, and Detective Lyons were anxiously waiting. The four rode out of town on different routes but met at the Guadalupe River border of the town, and then they headed to Seguin to execute the arrest warrant on Faust.

Deputy Schmidt asked, "So, what is the plan, Sheriff?"

Sheriff Saur said, "First we need to do this quietly, and then we will announce the arrest."

The others nodded, and Sheriff Saur continued, "It has been over two months since the murders, so I can imagine that he is not expecting the arrest. I do want you all to be on your toes. Deputy Schmidt, watch the back. Deputy Schultz, the west of the house; and Detective Lyons, take the east. I will knock on the front door and take him into custody. I have one question: What do you think we should do with Mrs. Faust? She can't be left alone."

Deputy Schmidt answered, "Mrs. Faust's sister just arrived from out of town and can take care of Mrs. Faust."

Sheriff Saur said, "All right, men, let's ride out."

The posse rode out to the Fausts' home a few miles from town, but this time nobody was outside to greet them. The men did as they were told, and Sheriff Saur knocked on the door.

A voice said, "Who is it?"

The sheriff yelled, "It is Sheriff Saur. I need to talk to you!"

Mr. Faust was not at home, and Mr. Rhodius asked, "Is everything okay, Sheriff?"

Mrs. Rhodius said, "I am taking care of Helen, Faust is not here. I believe he may be in Cibolo with Robert Hellmann or Seguin hiding out."

The sheriff tilted his hat and said, "Thank you, Mrs. Rhodius. We are looking for him."

Deputy Schmidt said, "I will ride out to Cibolo and scout ahead; he is probably at the inn in Seguin."

Sheriff Saur said, "Okay. I will take Detective Lyons and Schultz. If he is in Cibolo, just locate him, and we will come in and help with the arrest."

Deputy Schmidt rode toward the Cibolo, which was about halfway to San Antonio. Deputy Schmidt saw two young girls walking near the Cibolo. Deputy Schmidt was a well-known tracker and had hunted down many dangerous criminals.

He said, "Hello, ladies. I am a deputy sheriff with the Comal County Sheriff's office. Have you all seen a Mr. Faust?"

One of the little girls said, "Yes, that is my daddy's friend. He is fishing along the creek over there."

Deputy Schmidt looked toward the direction the girls pointed at and said, "Well, thank you all very much. You all have a nice day."

Deputy Schmidt tied his horse to a tree and walked down a steep embankment. He saw Mr. Hellman, who was a local Justice of the Peace, packing his things.

Deputy Schmidt said, "Afternoon, sir. I am Deputy Schmidt, and I am looking for Mr. Faust."

Mr. Hellman was doubtful and said, "Well, let me see your badge. I do not know you."

Deputy Schmidt lifted his flap on his vest and showed his badge to Mr. Hellman.

Mr. Hellman then asked, "What business do you have with Mr. Faust anyway?"

Deputy Schmidt said, "In case you have not heard, he is a suspect in a murder and the attempted murder of his wife."

Mr. Hellman looked annoyed and said, "I do not believe that. William would not do such a thing. You all need to leave him alone. You have a warrant?"

Deputy Schmidt replied, "In fact, yes, I do."

He handed the arrest warrant to Mr. Hellman, who said, "I guess this is serious. I will take you to him. I let him stay at my place."

Deputy Schmidt stopped at his brother-in-law's and asked him to ride to New Braunfels to get word that he had located Faust. Meanwhile, Deputy Schmidt followed Mr. Hellman to his home, where Faust had been staying.

Deputy Schmidt said, "Stand back. I will see if he is inside."

Deputy Schmidt opened the door and yelled, "Come on out, Mr. Faust. I have an arrest warrant for you!"

Deputy Schmidt noticed that nobody was inside and asked Mr. Hellman, "Where do you think he went?"

Mr. Hellman said, "I am not sure. He is usually just around the guesthouse. He might have gone to my store."

Deputy Schmidt got back on his horse and asked, "Which way to the store?"

Mr. Hellman pointed and said, "Follow the road, and you will run right into it."

Deputy Schmidt rode at full gallop and neared the feedstore. He quickly leaped off his horse and went inside the store. Deputy Schmidt looked around, and a loud crash of items knocked over startled his horse, and then the back door slammed shut. Deputy Schmidt ran out the back and saw William Faust running toward the creek.

Deputy Schmidt yelled, "William, stop. You are coming with me!"

William looked back and kept running. Deputy Schmidt drew his revolver, fired a shot, and yelled, "William, I will do what I have to do."

William stopped and put his hands up; Deputy Schmidt had caught his man and grabbed him by his arm.

William said, "What, you can't catch the murderer, so you are going to blame it on me?"

Deputy Schmidt said, "Just save it. You will have your day in court, you son of a bitch. Why aren't you looking for your wife's attacker?"

William said, "Easy for you to say. I know I am innocent."

Deputy Schmidt shackled and roped Faust like a roped calf and said, "Keep up with me, or I will hang you with that same rope."

William said, "You do that, and you will hang next. I will have the best attorneys representing me."

Deputy Schmidt continued to ride on his horse with William tied up with his hands shackled and attached by rope.

William yelled, "Where are you taking me? Comal County is the other way."

Deputy Schmidt looked back at William and did not say anything. He had a hard stare, one you would see from a man who had been through war and gunfights for most of his life. William looked into Deputy Schmidt's eyes and then looked away and was quiet. William knew if he tried anything, Deputy Schmidt would not hesitate for one second in killing him.

After riding about a half mile, they stopped at a school.

Deputy Schmidt pointed at William and said, "We are staying here till the posse brings a stagecoach for you. If you try anything, I will shoot you dead or take you all the way to town like this, or maybe I will just do both."

The school was empty, and Deputy Schmidt tied William to a chair. He also remained shackled at his hands and feet.

Deputy Schmidt looked at William and said, "It is tight … but you can get out, and I will chase you down and you will not make it to trial. I am the best tracker in South Texas; you won't get far, I promise."

William looked at Deputy Schmidt and said, "I am not going anywhere; you will be apologizing to me after the trial."

Deputy Schmidt said, "It will be dark soon, and I am going to sleep. I have nothing to say to you."

William looked at Deputy Schmidt as he sat on a chair and put his feet on the desk, tucking his hat. He was offended at his remark. William could not help it and said, "What makes you so sure that I killed Emma anyways?"

Deputy Schmidt tilted his hat up and looked at William, saying, "What did I tell you? I have nothing to say to you." Deputy Schmidt tilted his hat back down and shut his eyes.

William raised his voice and said, "It is because your sheriff is desperate and I am an easy target. This means you have nothing, so you are going to save your own asses."

Deputy Schmidt looked at William and said, "I have no problem getting on my horse and tying you up so you can walk as I ride back to New Braunfels; my horse knows the way, and I still will sleep. Besides, I have met many cold-blooded killers. Some are flat-out cowards who will shoot you in the back, but there are those few who will fight you face-to-face. I have met many; you are the coward who would shoot someone in the back."

William looked at Deputy Schmidt. He was shocked and said, "You are just wrong, Deputy; you are just wrong."

Deputy Schmidt tilted his head back, put his feet up, and said, "Now do you still want to talk, Mr. Faust?"

William made a face, and he chose wisely not to respond. Finally he tried to sleep, annoyed by Deputy Schmidt's response the rest of the night.

The next day the sheriff and his posse showed up in a wagon to transport William to the jail and bring him to face a judge and jury. The sheriff asked Deputy Schmidt, "Did he give you any problems?"

Schmidt looked at William and said, "Nope. He thought about running, but he knew I was not a woman or a child he could beat to death, so he surrendered quickly and knew I would have shot his ass in a heartbeat if he ran."

The sheriff looked at Deputy Schmidt and William and told William, "I guarantee you, we will not harm you unless you try to harm us. You will be brought to trial and have your day in court. Your life now depends on us because I guarantee you, there are lots of folks who want to kill you before you receive a fair trial."

William did not say a word. He looked at Deputy Schmidt and went into the wagon speechless.

• •

Sheriff Saur made clear his intentions to his posse. "Make sure he is protected at all times. Lyons, start the first watch and question him. I will let the editor know we have made an arrest on the case. Wilkins, take the next watch; and Schultz, you have the last one. Deputize a few more men that you trust to watch Mr. Faust. I want him watched twenty-four hours a day."

The sheriff walked to the editor's office and said to him, "We have made an arrest of Mr. Faust; a witness has identified him and has led us to overwhelming evidence to execute an arrest warrant."

The sheriff started back to his office across the street, and the editor said, "Wait, Sheriff. Is there anything more?"

The sheriff said, "That is enough for now. We will be in touch with further information and his upcoming court date."

• •

November 3, 1874

A meeting was called to prepare for Mr. Faust's habeas corpus hearing to set bail and to determine if there was enough evidence to hold him until his trial date, which would be at least a year away. The hearing would start on November 21 in the Texas Twenty-Second Judicial Court in front of the Honorable Judge John White. The prosecutor would be represented by John Ireland and W. H. Burgess. Mr. Faust had obtained well-known and well-funded attorneys representing him—Counsel Goodwin, Counsel Douglas, and Counsel Rust. Mrs. Faust and his sister provided the capital for Mr. Faust's prestigious legal team. The state prosecutors wished to meet with Detective Lyons and Sheriff Saur to go over the case.

Sheriff Saur and Detective Lyons went to the Comal County Courthouse across from the sheriff's office to meet with the state prosecutors. Sheriff Saur and the detective entered the room and noticed that John Ireland and Mr. Burgess were sitting at a table waiting for them.

The sheriff said, "Hello, I am Sheriff Saur, and this is my deputy, Detective Lyons."

The four shook hands, and they all were seated. Mr. Burgess was a man in his fifties, with a deep voice and a very serious look about him; Mr. Ireland was younger and seemed to be energetic and excited. Mr. Ireland said, "Well, let's start off with what we know we have on our side, and then I will address my concerns about the case."

Detective Lyons said, "First, we have a deceased thirteen-year-old child and a twenty-seven-year-old female with severe wounds. We have the murder weapon, which can be traced back to the crime; it has the initials WF, which stand for William Faust. We also have a medical record from Dr. Lehde who measured the wounds and the blade of the ax, which matches the impact area of the inflicted wounds. We also have a witness who led us to the ax and saw Mr. Faust fleeing the area after the crime was committed."

Mr. Burgess said, "Yes, this witness you mention, who is he?"

Sheriff Saur said, "He is a Negro man, a former slave named Isom Taylor, but he is solid on his recollection of the events, and the evidence of the ax corroborates his story."

Mr. Burgess said, "In a perfect world or maybe years from now, this may not matter, but the Civil War and the veterans are prominent in this area of the South and very likely to be on a jury."

Mr. Ireland said, "That is where I come in, Sheriff. I have worked with you on many cases. I just need your word and firm belief that your witness is solid."

Sheriff Saur said, "I would not have made an arrest in the case if I did not believe in this man. We cannot forget a child was horribly butchered."

Mr. Ireland said, "This is about justice, and I believe justice will prevail."

Mr. Burgess asked, "What does Mr. Faust have on his side, and are we going to speak to Mrs. Faust?"

Sheriff Saur looked at Detective Lyons and said, "I will let you explain this one."

Detective Lyons said, "Well, we have spoken to Mrs. Faust about what happened. We thought once she was away from Mr. Faust, she would change her mind. She said she will not testify for the prosecution and her husband would never do such a thing. She may testify for the defense."

Mr. Burgess sternly said, "Now let me get this straight. You made an arrest of Mr. Faust after the victim told you it was not him, and you are going to take the testimony of a Negro man to say otherwise. You expect us to keep him in jail and win a trial based on the only person alive who can name the perpetrator?"

Mr. Ireland said, "Remember, let's look at the facts of the case and similar cases. You know that a spouse rarely testifies against the other spouse, and we have the doctor's testimony, an innocent child who was murdered, and the murder weapon."

Mr. Burgess argued, "You said something very important, Mr. Ireland, and that is looking at the facts of the case. Will a judge, never mind you a jury, look past a Negro man's testimony against a white man's wife's testimony?"

Mr. Ireland said, "The truth and the facts will be brought out, and I think the only person who is lying is Mr. Faust, and we need to prove that. We do not need to prove Mrs. Faust is a liar or discredit her; she did not see much before the attack."

Mr. Burgess asked, "And, Sheriff, were you all able to get a confession?"

Detective Lyons said, "No, he is maintaining his innocence

but admits to being in Seguin, which we can verify; the witness saw him right after the murders."

Mr. Burgess and Mr. Ireland stood up, and Mr. Burgess said, "Well, it will be a miracle if we win; meanwhile, look for more evidence. I will not be surprised if the judge releases Mr. Faust and demands more evidence to warrant a trial."

Mr. Ireland said, "Well, this is not a trial. We just have to prove that there is enough evidence to charge Mr. Faust, and we have that. This is a habeas corpus hearing, so we will be ready. The trial will be at least one year away."

The sheriff said, "I understand, but what is right is right. We will see you in a few weeks."

November 21, 1874

The hearing was held at the Comal County Courthouse and filled with members of the community. Mr. Faust was brought in shackles and seated next to his attorneys. Mr. Burgess and Mr. Ireland were seated next to the Defense.

Deputy Schmidt shouted, "All rise. The Twenty-Second Judicial Court is now in session, the Honorable John White presiding."

Judge White spoke. "I realize we are full, but I expect order in this courtroom. This is not a trial but a hearing. The deputies will take you out of my courtroom if anyone cannot control their outbursts. You may all be seated.

The judge paused and said, "The State charges Mr. Faust with the murder of Emma Voelcker, a thirteen-year-old female, that took place on July 23, 1874."

The judge said, "Defense, do you wish to enter a plea now?"

Counsel Douglas, Rust, and Goodwin and Mr. Faust

stood up, and Counselor Douglas said, "We wish to enter a plea of not guilty, Your Honor."

The judge turned to the State and said, "What evidence do you have to hold Mr. Faust in custody?"

Mr. Burgess said, "The State provides evidence that on July 23, 1874, Emma Voelcker was murdered in her home and Mrs. Faust was brutally assaulted. We have testimony from two witnesses, Dr. Lehde and Isom Taylor, that can provide direct evidence of Mr. Faust as Emma Voelcker's murderer. We have recovered the murder weapon, this ax owned by Mr. Faust, and a doctor's testimony that the wounds were caused by that ax. Mr. Faust was seen leaving the scene of the crime by Isom Taylor."

The judge turned and said, "Defense, what is your argument to these accusations?"

Mr. Goodwin spoke for the Defense and said, "Your Honor, the evidence is circumstantial, and Mr. Faust should be released immediately to take care of his wife and protect her from the attacker if he was to return. The evidence is tainted by a former slave that is unhappy with Mr. Faust, and his testimony should not be entered in this case. Mrs. Faust has stated that Mr. Faust was not her attacker."

The judge asked, "What is the condition of Mrs. Faust, and where is she?"

Mr. Goodwin said, "She is still not well from the attack and not able to testify but getting better day by day, even though she will be blind the rest of her life."

The judge looked to the State and asked, "State, any rebuttal?"

Mr. Ireland said, "No, we believe there is substantial evidence to hold Mr. Faust for this horrible crime. The fact he is an escape risk could lead to letting her potential attacker free, placing her life in jeopardy."

Mr. Goodwin said, "Your Honor, this is purely circumstantial, and Mr. Faust should be let free based on insufficient evidence."

The judge looked at both sides and said, "Does either side have any other arguments?"

Mr. Ireland said, "No, the State rests."

Mr. Goodwin said, "The Defense rests."

The judge paused and looked at his notes. It was very quiet in the courtroom, and nobody spoke or moved, waiting on the judge's decision.

The judge said, "Based on the evidence presented, I find that there is enough evidence to hold Mr. Faust in jail to answer for the charges of murder."

Some of the audience cheered, and others protested. The judge paused, angrily banging his gavel, and said, "Order in this court, and furthermore, we will hold a trial next October, which will give enough time for the Defense to prepare their case and give Mrs. Faust ample time to recover."

Mr. Goodwin said, "Your Honor, Your Honor, can we at least have Faust placed in another jurisdiction since people have rushed to judgment?"

The judge narrowed his eyes at Mr. Goodwin and said, "I hope you are not insinuating that I rushed to judgment?"

Mr. Goodwin said, "No, Your Honor, just reacting to the community's mixed reactions when evidence has not been presented."

The judge paused and said, "I do concur, and discussions are now over. I order Mr. Faust to be transported to the Bexar County Jail for his protection."

Deputy Schmidt said, "All rise. Court has concluded."

The courtroom emptied, and the sheriff and Deputy Schultz took Mr. Faust back to his cell.

The judge said, "Let me have the State and Detective Lyons approach my bench."

They all approached the bench and Detective Lyons said, "Yes, Your Honor?"

The judge said, "I am going to warn you. During these trying times, you might want to find more evidence; it is enough to warrant a trial but not sure for a conviction."

They all looked at each other, and Detective Lyons said, "Yes, Your Honor."

Detective Lyons went back to the sheriff's office to talk to the sheriff about the judge's warning about the case.

The sheriff was waiting in his office and said, "Well, I guess that went well. We would have a riot on our hands if he'd released Faust."

Detective Lyons said, "The judge gave me a fair warning about making our case stronger."

The sheriff promised, "We will be ready. Get the order from the judge so we can transport Mr. Faust to San Antone in the morning."

CHAPTER 9

DETECTIVE LYONS'S QUEST FOR A CONFESSION

The work slowed after the hectic few months of the events of Emma Voelcker's murder. Thanksgiving, Christmas, and the New Year had passed, and it was now a month into 1875. As February began, Detective Lyons thought long and hard about the case and the upcoming trial in October. He ruminated on what the judge had told him about the case.

He knew in his heart and mind that William Faust had murdered Emma. It fell to him to turn up new evidence, and he had to think of a way how. He knew that William Faust had been jailed for over three months. Detective Lyons woke up in the middle of the night thinking of this case and how he had been unsuccessful in compelling Faust to confess. Suddenly he had an idea; somehow, he wanted a man, good or bad, to feel what he was feeling on this case. Detective Lyons began a letter, a letter to the man jailed with Faust, to plead for help in obtaining a confession. The letter read:

> Dear Sir,
> I know you probably have never thought of helping the law; you might consider me

your sworn enemy but I am not. There is a mutual respect and even a code of honor among the criminal world. I know testifying against a fellow jail mate and aiding the law is not in this code of honor. But there is a time to put all things aside and put yourself in another light or life as a big brother, father, or uncle. Think of a man who would kill a kid with an ax and then kill his wife.

These were victims: a father in mourning, a mother, a sister, an aunt, an entire family devastated because of one cowardly, greedy act. I respect you as outlaws, but I do not respect this coward for hiding among you. I plead to you to do the right thing and obtain a confession, not for me but for this family and child. Show that even though you are accused of crimes, you are still human beings. I cannot offer any reward or reduction of jail time or sympathy for your actions. I can just respect you as men, men who deal with each other in your own code of honor that I know exists. I plead to you to assist and write a statement that comes from his words. If he is not guilty of any crime, then I expect you to tell me that so I do not pursue an innocent man. This murder was cold, and the evil being does not deserve to be among either free or imprisoned men.

Sincerely,
Detective Lyons

Detective Lyons finally went back to bed and fell asleep after writing the letter. He rode to the sheriff's office to discuss his plan with the sheriff the next day.

Detective Lyons said, "Sheriff, I have an idea that you may not like, but if it works, we may have something we desperately need."

Sheriff Saur had his feet on his desk, and he said, "Oh boy, go on."

Detective Lyons said, "I need to go to San Antonio and deliver this letter to jailed mates who have been housed with Faust. Here is the letter. Read it."

The sheriff read the letter. Then he scratched his head and said, "You know, at first I did not like it, but if it works, it may open up more leads; go ahead and go."

Detective Lyons said, "All right, I am on my way. I am going to stay in San Antonio for a few days just in case I get a response. I would really like to interview each cellmate to see if they can even read this letter."

Sheriff Saur said, "That is fine, but be careful and do not let anyone know what you are doing. The tension is still high about this."

Detective Lyons rode on horseback to San Antonio, where Mr. Faust was being held in the Bexar County Jail. Detective Lyons made his way inside the jail and was met by a Bexar County jailer.

Detective Lyons said, "Good afternoon. I am Deputy Detective Lyons from Comal County, and you are holding Mr. Faust."

The deputy said, "Afternoon. I am Deputy Johnson. I am familiar with Mr. Faust."

Detective Lyons said, "Has he said anything to anyone as far as his case goes?"

The deputy replied, "Nope. He only talks to his lawyers and his jail buddies."

Detective Lyons said, "I have a request. I need to speak with jail mates who have had contact with him, and if you could set me up with a place to talk to them in private."

The deputy said, "I can arrange that, but they aren't going to talk to the law."

Detective Lyons said, "I understand, but this has to be done. And is there is anyplace I can stay for a few nights?"

The deputy said, "We have some bunks in the next room for deputies. You can use one as long as you like. I will go get you the first bunkmate, Alexander Allen. You can use my desk."

Detective Lyons sat at the deputy's desk and retrieved his letter from his bag. The deputy brought in Mr. Allen, a short man in his late twenties. He had a rough, weathered face for his age that showed exposure to years of windburn and sunburn.

Detective Lyons said, "Have a seat."

Mr. Allen said, "I would rather not sit; this isn't going to take long."

Detective Lyons said, "Just to let you know, I am not interested in what you are accused of, and I am not going to ask you about a new crime or anything like that, so just have a seat."

Mr. Allen took a seat and said, "What's this about then?"

Detective Lyons said, "This is about Mr. Faust, your cell mate, not you."

Mr. Allen said, "I don't have anything to say about him or myself."

Detective Lyons pulled out his letter and said, "Let me read you this letter, and we will be done, I promise; I'm just asking you to listen."

Detective Lyons read the letter that he had written for Faust's jail mates.

Mr. Allen did not say anything and sat on his chair as if he were holding a burning question.

Detective Lyons asked, "Did you have any questions?"

Mr. Allen said, "Is that the way it really went down, or are you trying to make us turn on one another?"

Detective Lyons said, "Look, like I said, you do not have to do anything at all. I will be in town for a few days, so if you want to talk, let me know."

Mr. Allen said, "All right; let me think about this."

Detective Lyons said, "I am sorry I cannot offer you anything on your case or your charges, but this is all I came for."

The deputy took Mr. Allen back to his cell, and Detective Lyons said, "Let me see if that gets me anywhere. I am going to grab a drink and a bite and come back and call it a day."

• •

The next morning Detective Lyons was woken early by a new deputy taking the shift over. The deputy said, "Detective Lyons, Mr. Allen has been asking to speak with you."

Detective Lyons said, "Thank you, I will get ready and meet you in the office."

Detective Lyons got ready and saw that the deputy and Mr. Allen were already in the office.

The deputy said, "I will be in the front when you need me."

Detective Lyons asked, "So, you asked to see me, Mr. Allen. It's kind of early."

Mr. Allen said, "Well, I thought about what you said, and when you are locked in jail, that seems to be all you can do is think. Faust did tell me some things; he claims killing the girl was an accident."

Detective Lyons could not believe what he was hearing, Mr. Faust had admitted to someone that he had killed Emma!

Detective Lyons said, "Well, I respect you as a man for telling me this. Let's talk as men and not as a lawman to an accused man. I need to know everything and if you're willing to swear to it. I will write down what you say and read it to you, and after that, if you feel it is something you want to say, I will have you swear to it."

Mr. Allen began to talk, and Detective Lyons wrote as he spoke,

"Mr. Faust told me two nights ago; we had been in the same cell for a few weeks. He said that he started from a Stagecoach Inn in Seguin around eleven. He said he was met on the road by some Negro man, who he said did not think he would recognize him. He said he arrived in New Braunfels at nearly 1:00 a.m. He told me he then entered the back door near the room where his wife and the little girl slept. He told me he went in there to kill his wife and only his wife, but that kid woke up and saw him; he claimed he had to kill her to hide his crime. He told me in confidence that since we were both jail mates, he could trust me. He claimed not to fear being hanged. An arrangement with a friend was made to murder his wife, and they would split the money after he married his wife's sister. They were going to go to Mexico after that. The friend failed to do his part, so he ended up trying to kill her himself. He then left and rode back to Seguin and got there at about five. Before he got to Seguin, he burned his clothes and threw the ax in the river. He said he saw the Negro male still fishing, but he was riding so fast there was no way he could be recognized. He pledged that he was going to beat this case or be released and break me out to flee to Mexico."

Detective Lyons asked, "Is there anything else?"

Mr. Allen said, "No, not from me. He is full of shit and yellow."

Detective Lyons asked, "What do you mean not from me?"

Mr. Allen said, "There are two more of us who want to talk to you. I have no sympathy for that son of a bitch. He will get what he deserves."

Detective Lyons said, "Thank you. Who are the other two?"

Mr. Allen said, "Jason Lee and Johnny Williams, they have more to tell. That is all I can swear to him telling me, and I cannot speak for the others. That Faust does not belong with us. You're right; move him out of my cell before I kill him myself."

Detective Lyons said, "I will let the family have closure on the truth. I will get him moved out of there."

The jailer came in and escorted Mr. Allen back to the cell. Then he said, "I will be back with Mr. Lee."

When Mr. Lee walked in, Detective Lyons saw he also was a man in his late twenties. He had more of a younger yet rougher look than Mr. Allen but a very stocky build.

Detective Lyons said, "Have a seat, Mr. Lee. I appreciate you coming in."

Mr. Lee said, "You know, nobody has ever called me mister. It's always thief, crook, hey you, but never mister."

Detective Lyons said, "I have no reason to judge you or investigate you; I am actually coming to you for help, so please tell me what you know."

Mr. Lee began his testimony and said, "About a week ago, I told Mr. Faust to not tell anyone anything that would incriminate him on his case. I have had a lot of thoughts on how to deal with someone I just do not respect. I thought about cutting his throat, but there is no honor in that. I am a man, and I have had other problems with other men; the choice was made to tangle, and obviously I am here to pay for my choices. When it comes to a child, there is nothing that would warrant a killing of a wife or child like the way he did. Now to tell you what he told me. He claimed that there was another man who was supposed to help him murder his wife, but he never showed. His wife's family had come into some money, and he was going to kill her, get the money, and split it with this other man, but he fled for Old Mexico. He was then going to marry into the family again to get the rest of the money. Faust said he knew you were on his trail, but he was smarter than you.

"He admitted that you were on the right track. He said he got up just after eleven at the Stagecoach Inn and made sure nobody saw him slip out. He made sure he was back by five before anyone saw him. Nobody saw him, and he burned the clothes, so he did not have them in the hotel; he said they were covered with blood. The girl woke up and recognized him, and he swung his ax on his way out of the room. The ax was an old meat ax he had. He said he made a big mistake when that Negro Taylor saw him on the way back to Seguin. He made a mistake and should have acted like he was hunting the murderer instead of hiding out. He said he should have killed the Negro man but decided not to because nobody would believe him."

Detective Lyons said, "Is there anything else?"

Mr. Lee looked down and said, "I might as well tell you. He admitted to killing another person."

Detective Lyons, curious, asked, "Who is it that he also killed?"

Mr. Lee replied, "Faust claims he killed a Dr. Rhein."

Detective Lyons was shocked but contained his emotions at this break in the case, simply saying, "So, tell me about this murder."

Lee went on. "Faust told me the doctor borrowed his horse

to exchange some money in San Antonio. He dug a shallow grave in the back of his pharmacy, but it stank badly. He then took the body and the horse and buried the body near Salado. He then sold the horse to a Negro man. He told me he got two thousand dollars out of the entire murder. Faust admitted that he had murdered many times and always felt that if something needed to be done, he would do it himself."

Detective Lyons asked, "Is there anything else you want to say?"

Mr. Lee said, "Personally, I respect a man who kills another man because of a quarrel, and it is settled between the two. I have no respect for a man who kills a woman or child. Faust has admitted to murdering many more; he has not told me about them in detail, but he admitted to doing so."

Detective Lyons said, "Thank you, Mr. Lee."

The jailer took Mr. Lee back and went to get the final cellmate, Mr. John Williams.

When the jailer brought in John Williams, Detective Lyons saw he was a tall male in his late thirties.

John Williams said, "How are you doing, Detective? I am just going to be upfront. I am a career criminal, so I have no time for bullshit. I overheard this Faust conversation with Allen. Faust thought I was asleep when he was talking to Allen, but I was not. I heard Faust tell Allen that he killed his wife first and then the girl. I heard him say that he ran into the Negro man about six miles from Seguin; that is all I remember. That is all I should say. I don't care for that sumbitch. He isn't no criminal in my book; he is a yellow-bellied coward."

Mr. Williams did not say anything else, but it was important to confirm that Faust did have a conversation with Lee about the murders.

Detective Lyons said, "Thank you," and the deputy came to escort Mr. Williams back to his cell. Detective Lyons said,

"Deputy, I am going back to New Braunfels today. Thank you for your help."

The deputy responded, "Anytime."

Detective Lyons got his belongings together and rode off to New Braunfels to inform the sheriff of his new findings, hoping it would make the case stronger.

• •

Back in New Braunfels, Detective Lyons briefed Sheriff Saur on his findings.

Sheriff Saur said, "You know, I am impressed, getting these guys who have a code not to tell the law anything. These guys didn't ask for any favors?"

Detective Lyons replied, "No, Sheriff. I was surprised I got a quick response. I am not sure if there is anything else we can do. I think all witnesses and possible witnesses came forward. I believe all are truthful, and we have the murder weapon with his initials on it. I will keep an eye on all witnesses and make sure Isom Taylor is safe. I need to speak to the sheriff in Guadalupe County; he told me that Isom is an honest man and he would vouch for him."

The sheriff said, "We have done the best we can, and we have a solid case. There is nothing we can do except wait for the trial to come. I may retire before that time; this case has taken a toll on me."

PART II
THE TRIAL

CHAPTER 10

THE TRIAL BEGINS

October 13, 1875

Isom Taylor was nervous and hesitant as he was walking. He stopped and looked at the courthouse, debating whether or not he should go inside. But he knew what he had to do: tell the truth. He knew that many in the country would still not see him as an equal person speaking against a white man. The Civil War had ended slavery, but it did not end the way people would still think. People in the South did not necessarily agree with the outcome of the war, even though they had to abide by the new laws of the land. For his part, Isom saw himself not as a black man or a former slave, but as an honest man who saw men as men on the same platform no matter their wealth, status, or race.

If Isom did not stand up for himself or others like him, a child's murderer, regardless of color, would go free. Little did Isom realize that testifying in a courtroom was the toughest thing he would do in his life; many fellow black men told him to not worry about the white people's problems. To Isom, this meant that even though a bloody civil war had been waged, largely over the issue of slavery, simply not exercising his rights would be dishonorable to those who fell. For the many reasons that went through Isom's mind, despite the political issues, testifying was nonetheless the right thing to do.

As mentioned, Isom had been told by his friends to let the white people figure out their own problems and stay out of the trial, or there would be problems. Yet Isom only saw himself as a father who lost his daughter to an evil man, not as a former soldier; he had hope that one day the hatred of a nation over the recent conflagration would come to a rest. He would stand for what was right and would hope for now that starting with the small town of New Braunfels, the rest of the country would ultimately follow.

It was standing room only more than a year after the death of young Emma in the Twenty-Second Judicial District Court in front of special sitting judge, the Honorable Judge E. Altgelt of San Antonio, Texas. District Attorney John O. Walker was assigned to prosecute the case. Mr. Faust was represented by a Seguin native, Captain Rust, a well-respected attorney in the state of Texas. Judge Altgelt had not taken the bench yet, and the crowd quieted as William Faust was escorted by Sheriff Saur and Detective Lyons. Faust's legal team now consisted only of Captain Rust due to diminishing funds, and Prosecutor Walker was the sole prosecutor for the trial phase.

Deputy Schmidt was the acting bailiff, and the lawman escorted the infamous accused murderer to his counsel, who was seated at the defense table. Deputy Schmidt then escorted Judge E. Altgelt into the courtroom and, taking his position standing to the left of the bench, called out in a loud voice, "All rise. The Twenty-Second Judicial District Court is now in session; the Honorable Judge Altgelt is presiding." Judge Altgelt was a large man who wore glasses and carried his Bible into the courtroom; he used his index finger to push his glasses up as he looked at a standing room only courtroom and sat at the bench.

Judge Altgelt said, "Thank you, Deputy Schmidt. Ladies and gentlemen, please be seated. Bring in the jury, so I can swear them in."

Captain Rust blurted out, "Your Honor, we would first like to request a hearing to dismiss the charges based on insufficient evidence."

Judge Altgelt looked at Captain Rust and said, "First, you will need to stand up when you address this court, Counselor."

Captain Rust said, "Your Honor, I am sorry. Can I approach and discuss this before the jury is brought in?"

Judge Altgelt looked up and said, "Both sides approach; Counsel, what is your concern?"

Captain Rust said, "Well, Your Honor, I am sure you have received and read the briefs that properly point out that the prosecution's witness does not have a valid claim as a citizen and cannot testify against my client."

Judge Altgelt asked, "Which witness are you referring to and what basis?"

Captain Rust replied, "Why, of course, Mr. Isom Taylor. He is a former slave, and although he is free, he does not have a right to testify or be held on the same status as other witnesses."

Judge Altgelt looked at Prosecutor Walker and said, "Obviously this case law has changed. The South lost the Civil War ten years ago, and this is a jury trial, which will determine the validity of each witness's testimony. I will allow the testimony."

Captain Rust was upset and asked, "Have you considered a change of venue? My client cannot receive a fair trial in New Braunfels."

Judge Altgelt replied, "This case is well known throughout

71

Texas. The telegraph has put the story out from New York to California and every Texas town. Do you recall the governor in Austin offered a reward? He was housed in San Antone. A change of venue would be pointless. Your motions are denied, and bailiff, bring in the jury so I can swear them in."

Captain Rust returned to his table and under his breath grumbled, "Well, I guess that gives me my first reason for appeal."

Deputy Schmidt escorted the jury into the courtroom and in a raised voice said, "All rise for the jury."

Twelve jurymen marched into the courtroom. They were Henry Dirks, Adolph Penshorn, H. W. Boehm, Wenzel Nowotny, John Marschall, Joseph Pfeiffer, Franz Nowotny, Andreas Pape, Peter Nowotny, Christian Guenther, Peter Daum, and Max Tausch. All were hardworking men, some farmers and some business owners. Three Nowotnys, who were all cousins, were all on the jury. Mr. Faust stared at the men as they approached, realizing that his fate was in their hands.

The judge said, "Before we begin, I expect order in my courtroom from all, which includes counselors, witnesses, and spectators in this public trial. Now, other than the gentlemen of the jury, all others please be seated." After the others sat, the judge said, "Gentlemen of the jury, raise your right hand and repeat after me. Do each of you solemnly swear to our Almighty God that you will and truly try, in good faith, in the case of the State of Texas versus William Faust, to render a true verdict according to the law and the evidence, so help you God?"

They all replied in the affirmative, and the judge instructed them to be seated.

The judge then looked at William Faust and said, "Would the accused please rise."

Faust and his defense counsel stood up.

"Mr. Faust, you are accused of one count of murder and one count of attempted murder. How do you wish to plea?"

Captain Rust stated, "Not guilty, Your Honor."

The judge said, "You may be seated. State, you may start your opening statement."

Prosecutor Walker stood up and walked to the jury box. "Thank you, Your Honor. Gentlemen of the jury, this is a simple case of cold-blooded murder. The prosecution will show that a young lady, Emma Voelcker, was brutally murdered, and Mrs. Faust was nearly savagely murdered, losing her sight for the rest of her life. The state will show the facts and the investigation that point to the one and only person, or must I say devil, William Faust." Walking to the defense table and pointing, Prosecutor Walker continued, "The evidence is irrefutable, but the Defense will put in your head a history lesson and bring up our nation's most horrible war. I will urge you not to buy into this; you will see the truth that a young lady is dead. An innocent wife has been conned and battered, and remember that there is good and evil in this world, not black or white. Let me say this again: there is good and evil in this world, and it is not black or white; good and evil have no color. It is your duty to weigh this evidence and look at the facts, evidence, and testimony of the honorable men, women, and lawmen who will swear to our one and only God to tell the truthful accounts of what happened. Thank you, gentlemen."

The judge then stated, "Defense, you may proceed with your opening statement."

Captain Rust said, "Thank you, Your Honor. Good morning, gentlemen of the jury and Your Honor. Let me remind you that you all have sworn an oath to determine the truth. This is a highly publicized case, in which the prosecution and lawmen were pressured to bring forth a suspect for what I agree is a horrible crime." Pointing at the prosecutor's table, he continued, "I assure you Mr. William Faust is an honorable man accused of this horrible crime that he did not commit. You will hear testimony for the prosecution from men and women who were not even there when the crime took place. More importantly, you will hear testimony from an eyewitness who will testify that it was not Mr. Faust who assaulted Mrs. Faust or killed little Emma Voelcker. The prosecution will desperately introduce questionable evidence, testimony from violent outlaws, and perhaps be desperate enough to put a former slave on the stand to give testimony. I ask you not to buy into the prosecution's ploy to simply make this case go away and send an innocent man to his death. The real killer is still on the loose and will likely murder once again. Gentlemen, you have been chosen to seek the truth and not to condemn an innocent man, and even though it is not my burden to show you the proof—that is the prosecution's task—I will respond with the truth, which unfortunately does not put this puzzle of a crime together although the prosecution will desperately try to convince you to believe their fabrications and misrepresentations. Why? Because there are pieces missing that simply do not add up, and you will see there is a lack of evidence or no evidence at all, just these remarkable theories that are without proof. There will be a lot of emotion here, but I ask all of you to weigh the evidence, not the emotion. Thank you, gentlemen."

The judge looked at the Defense and said, "Very well." Then he turned to the prosecution. "Mr. Walker, call your first witness."

The prosecutor stood up and said, "Your Honor, we call Deputy Schmidt."

Deputy Schmidt relinquished his court duties to Deputy Homann to testify on the stand. Deputy Schmidt approached the bench and stood beside the judge.

The judge said, "Raise your right hand and place your left hand on the Bible. Do you swear to tell the truth, the whole truth, and nothing but the truth, so help you God?"

Deputy Schmidt replied, "I do, Your Honor."

The judge said, "Thank you, Deputy. You may be seated."

Prosecutor Walker stood up and said, "Morning, Deputy. Can you tell the jury your job title and your experience as a deputy sheriff?"

Deputy Schmidt responded, "During the Civil War, I was a tracker and a scout. When the war ended, Sheriff Saur asked me to work for him. I have been a deputy sheriff for ten years and tracked down hundreds of outlaws who have murdered, robbed banks, and robbed trains."

Prosecutor Walker asked, "At what point were you first assigned to the Emma Voelcker murder case, and what were you tasked to do?"

Deputy Schmidt answered, "Well, it started on the morning of July 23 last year. Sheriff Saur told me that Emma Voelcker and Mrs. Faust were attacked, and both would probably be dead by nightfall."

Prosecutor Walker asked, "Did you go to the Voelcker home and see the crime scene?"

"Yes, sir, I did."

"What did you see?"

Deputy Schmidt took a breath, looked down, and spoke. "I have seen a lot of blood in my life—during the war, murder investigations, and taking down outlaws when I had to. I had never seen that much blood splashed on the wall and never seen a young child intentionally bludgeoned in such a way. I have always seen soldiers, lawmen, and outlaws dead but never a child murdered."

Prosecutor Walker then asked, "What was your part in the investigation and apprehension of Mr. Faust?"

Captain Rust stood up and said, "I object to this form of questioning. It is conclusive and leading."

Judge Altgelt said, "He is simply asking what was his part of the investigation and apprehension. Overruled. Deputy, you may answer the question."

Deputy Schmidt said, "I would say once Sheriff Saur's investigation was complete, I was given the task to track and locate Mr. Faust on a warrant for his arrest that was issued."

"Can you identify Mr. Faust for the jury?"

Deputy Schmidt pointed to Faust and said, "It is the man with a white shirt and black coat sitting across from me."

Faust stared at Schmidt, and the deputy stared back at him until he looked down as his intimidation attempt failed.

Prosecutor Walker asked, "Where did you pick up Faust's trail?"

"I found him west of Cibolo Creek."

Prosecutor Walker then asked, "Deputy Schmidt, can you tell us how you tracked him near the Cibolo?"

Deputy Schmidt replied, "Sure. Sheriff Saur took half of his posse to look for Faust in Seguin, and I was tasked to check Cibolo due to Mr. Faust's mother-in-law giving information he might be there."

Prosecutor Walker asked, "When you got near Cibolo, what information did you receive that he was there?"

"I saw two young ladies near Cibolo Creek and asked if they had seen or knew a Mr. Faust. One of the ladies said that he was a friend of her daddy, who was fishing nearby; she pointed toward him. When I approached Mr. Hellman, he asked me my business; I identified myself, and he demanded to see a warrant. After I showed the warrant, he said he would take me to his house; he had let Faust stay there."

"Was he at the house?"

Deputy Schmidt answered, "No. When I asked Mr.

Hellman where Faust might be, he suggested he might have gone to Hellman's Feedstore. When I got there, Faust saw me. He ran, and I caught him and told him he was under arrest."

Prosecutor Walker next asked, "So he ran from you, did he tell you why?"

Deputy Schmidt replied, "Faust told me that I should be looking for his wife's attacker."

"What did you tell him?"

"I told him I was looking for the murderer, and I found him."

For a moment, the courtroom began whispering after Schmidt had answered. Judge Altgelt immediately slammed his gavel and yelled, "There will be order in this court!"

Prosecutor Walker asked, "Did he resist?"

"No, he came willingly after I fired a warning shot and told him he was coming with me one way or another."

Prosecutor Walker asked, "Do innocent men usually try to run from you, Deputy?"

"No, never."

Prosecutor Walker nodded as if approving of the reply and then said, "I have no further questions for this witness."

Judge Altgelt looked at Captain Rust and said, "Your witness."

Captain Rust stood and said sharply to Schmidt, "Morning, Deputy. I have a few questions if that is okay."

Schmidt replied, "Go ahead, sir."

Captain Rust said, "My first question is what else did my client say to you when you arrested him?"

Schmidt said, "He told me that I should be looking for his wife's killer."

Captain Rust said, "I understand that, but did Mr. Faust say that he was innocent?"

Schmidt almost smiled. "Oh yeah, he did; they always say that."

The audience and jury chuckled at Schmidt's comment.

Captain Rust was irritated. His face turned red, and he quickly blurted out, "Deputy, I am referring to my client on that day. Answer the question."

Schmidt now sounded stoic. "Yes, he told me he was innocent."

Captain Rust said, "And at any time did you see my client commit an assault on his wife or kill young Emma Voelcker?"

"No, I did not."

Captain Rust said, "You just simply executed an arrest warrant on Mr. Faust based on another party's observations?"

"Yes."

Captain Rust said, "I have no more questions, Your Honor."

Judge Altgelt asked, "State, do you have any redirect questions?"

Prosecutor Walker replied, "No, Your Honor, not for Deputy Schmidt. The State calls its next witness, Justice of the Peace of Guadalupe County Robert Hellman."

Robert Hellman was sworn in and took a seat on the witness stand.

Prosecutor Walker asked, "Mr. Hellman, can you introduce yourself to the members of the jury?"

Robert Hellman said, "My name is Robert Hellman. I am the Justice of the Peace for Guadalupe County."

"Can you explain how you know Mr. Faust and how long you have known him?"

Robert Hellman answered, "Well, I have known Mr. Faust for the past seven years. I conducted the marriage in my courtroom with Mr. Faust and his wife Helen about a year before this incident."

Prosecutor Walker then asked, "Did you know that Mr. Faust was a fugitive when Deputy Schmidt came to arrest him?"

Robert Hellman responded, "No, I did not."

Prosecutor Walker asked, "Were you helping hide Mr. Faust in any way?"

Robert Hellman seemed to stiffen a bit. "I was not."

"Did Mr. Faust tell you he was fleeing from authorities in Comal County and Guadalupe County when he was apprehended by Deputy Schmidt?"

Robert Hellman said, "He did. I was there to give him advice and advised him to turn himself in."

Prosecutor Walker asked, "In your experience, how many innocent persons have you seen flee from the law?"

Captain Rust stood up and said, "Your Honor, I object to this line of questioning. The Honorable Mr. Hellman is not on trial here."

Prosecutor Walker looked at the judge and said, "I will withdraw the question, Your Honor. I have no more questions."

Judge Altgelt looked at Captain Rust. "Counsel?"

Captain Rust said, "No, Your Honor. The Honorable Mr. Hellman has answered the questions he needed to answer."

Judge Altgelt said, "You may step down subject to recall if needed." He then hit his gavel and said, "Let's break for lunch. Bailiff, escort the jury to across the street, and we will call for the next witness after lunch. Be back here at one o'clock."

The bailiff called out, "All rise. Court will be back in session in one hour."

There was a lot of whispering among the audience in the courtroom, and the jury followed the bailiff across the street. A table was already prepared for the twelve and one for the bailiff. The bailiff said, "There is a menu prepared for the next few days here at this inn. I was told that you will be sequestered until the trial is over. You are not to discuss the trial with anyone until it is time and it is over."

The men sat down to eat and were served lunch. There were many people from the trial and others just passing by looking at them through a window, with some outright staring. For their part, the jury members all sat quietly, and finally Franz Nowotny spoke up. "Bailiff, this is a first time for us, and many of us have duties to perform at home. I am sure we all need to know what to expect from this trial."

The bailiff replied, "Well, they said the testimony may last all week, and that is when all twelve of you have to elect a foreman and come to a unanimous decision on guilt or innocence. If you cannot reach a decision, and that means if one or more of you disagree, then it is a mistrial. If you all agree, then the judge will hear your verdict."

Franz looked at his fellow jurors and asked, "Does anyone want the task of foreman?"

Wenzel and Peter Nowotny looked at each other and laughed. Peter said, "Cousin, looks like you just volunteered yourself."

Franz looked at the jurors at the table, and they nodded their heads in agreement. Franz said, "I will agree if there are no objections."

The bailiff finished chewing his food and said, "I will let the judge know when the time is right. Let me know if you change your mind."

The jurors did not say much more for the first day and finished their lunch in time to return to the courtroom. The bailiff led the jurors to the courtroom, and the judge was already on the bench. The bailiff proclaimed, "All rise for the jury and the courtroom!" The whispering ceased as everybody's attention focused back on the trial.

Judge Altgelt asked, "Who is the next witness?"

Prosecutor Walker stood and said, "The State calls Sheriff Saur."

The doors opened to the courtroom, and Sheriff Saur walked in. All eyes were on the local Comal County Sheriff.

Judge Altgelt swore the sheriff in, and the veteran lawman sat like a pro facing the jury, looking very relaxed.

Prosecutor Walker asked, "Can you state your name and title for the jury?"

Sheriff Saur cleared his throat and said, "I am the current sheriff of Comal County, and my name is Sheriff Saur."

"Can you identify Mr. William Faust in the courtroom?"

The sheriff turned from the jury, pointed to the defense table where Faust was sitting, and said, "Yeah, he is right there in the white shirt and black pants."

Both Faust and the sheriff stared at each other, and the sheriff continued to point at him like two dominant dogs that refused to take their eyes off each other before a fight.

Prosecutor Walker cleared his throat, and the sheriff continued to stare until Faust finally looked away. Sheriff Saur turned to face Prosecutor Walker and partially faced toward the jury.

"Sheriff, can you tell us about the night and early morning of July 22 and 23 in the year of our Lord 1874?"

Sheriff Saur replied, "Sure. It is a night I will never forget. I was alerted by Mr. Voelcker, who told me that Mrs. Faust and his daughter, Emma, had been murdered. I alerted Deputy Schmidt, and we both rode to the Voelckers home. When we arrived, Mrs. Faust's dogs continually barked at us before we even entered the home. Mr. Voelcker had to put the dogs away so we could hear ourselves talk."

Prosecutor Walker asked, "What did you see once you arrived at the Voelcker home?"

The sheriff looked straight ahead, staring at the doors to

the courtroom in deep thought with a face of shock, and said, "I saw blood, sir."

Prosecutor Walker asked, "Where was this blood coming from?"

Sheriff Saur closed his eyes and opened them, looking at the Voelcker family in sadness. He said, "The blood was coming from Emma Voelcker and Mrs. Faust, I have seen a lot of blood in my lifetime but never from the deliberate butchering of a child."

The audience whispered, and some were horrified of the memory this testimony brought back. The judge ordered the courtroom to be silent.

Prosecutor Walker said, "Can you describe the injuries on the victims?"

The sheriff said, "I did not recognize Mrs. Faust at first because her face was full of fresh and dry blood on her forehead, and her hair was blood soaked. There seemed to be one vicious blow to her forehead. Young Emma ..."

The sheriff paused as he had learned to put thoughts away in the back of his mind until it was time to remember. Sheriff Saur then said, "Young Emma had several blows to the front and back of her head; I assumed it was young Emma. Mr. Voelcker confirmed that it was her. Both were bleeding badly, and only Mrs. Faust was breathing slightly. I was sure Emma was dead and thought Mrs. Faust would soon be."

Prosecutor Walker asked, "Mrs. Faust wasn't dead yet?'

Sheriff Saur answered, "Mrs. Faust was in a coma but alive. She eventually recovered but was blinded in both eyes for life."

"Sheriff Saur, did you have any witnesses or suspects?"

"At the time of the murder investigation, we had no witnesses or suspects. I put a watch of an eight-man posse to round up anyone suspicious and ease the tension in town; folks were frightened."

"Sheriff, please summarize the details of the investigation"—Prosecutor Walker then walked toward the defense table, pointed at Faust, raised his voice, and added—"and how it led to the arrest of that man, Mr. William Faust!"

Sheriff Saur answered, "Initially we did not have any suspects, but we had a key witness come forward. He identified Faust fleeing the area right after the crime. We also found a key piece of evidence that belonged to Mr. Faust."

Captain Rust stood up and said, "I object to this line of questioning. No weapon has been introduced as evidence, and the witness he is speaking of has not testified or been identified."

Prosecutor Walker responded, "Judge, I am merely asking the sheriff about his personal knowledge. We will be introducing the weapon and the witness."

Judge Altgelt answered, "I will allow it. I am sure we are going to get to the witness and the weapon."

Sheriff Saur continued, "We also noticed that Mr. Faust did not assist with the apprehension or investigation of his wife's assailant."

Prosecutor Walker asked, "Why would you consider his lack of involvement in his wife's murder investigation suspicious?"

Sheriff Saur turned, stared at Faust, and answered, "Well, I know I would hunt down my wife's assailant and the murderer of an innocent child until I could not walk or ride or was shot. I think any *man* who loved his wife would protect her and avenge her. We had to hunt down Faust like any other murderer or robber, and instead of helping, he tried to escape like a criminal."

Prosecutor Walker asked, "Sheriff Saur, would you agree

that you managed this investigation and apprehension of Mr. Faust?"

"Yes, I oversaw the case in its entirety."

The prosecutor then said, "I have no more questions, Your Honor."

Judge Altgelt looked at the Defense and said, "Your witness."

Captain Rust glanced at some notes and then made eye contact with Sheriff Saur. "Sheriff, I know you have an impeccable record as a peace officer in Comal County, and you are very respected in Comal County."

Sheriff Saur replied, "I would like to think that respectable people favor me and the not-so-respectable do not. Not sure if you count on either side, so I will not say thank you for your compliment just yet."

"Obviously it is the jury that must decide," Captain Rust retorted. "I want to ask you if you were under incredible pressure to find a murderer."

"I always put pressure on myself to find a murderer and to protect this town from any danger. After all, that is my job."

"But did you feel incredible pressure from the county commissioners, who put up a five-hundred-dollar reward, and even further pressure after the governor's office matched the award?"

Sheriff Saur leaned forward and looked around, saying, "Obviously you did not hear me, and it looks like everyone but you did hear me. I put pressure on myself to find every murderer. What do you think? I sit across the street with my feet on my desk waiting for a crime to solve itself?"

Captain Rust remained calm even after the crowd chuckled and the judge yelled once again for order in the courtroom.

Captain Rust continued, "So, the pressure from the state and local government that had all eyes on Comal County never put any stress on you to simply pick a suspect everyone would presumably believe, which led to a poor circumstantial investigation?"

"I have already answered your question, Counsel, I am sorry you do not like my answer."

Captain Rust persisted. "So, you have made it clear that you were under pressure to find a suspect to ease the pressure off yourself."

Sheriff Saur moved in his chair as if preparing to snap at Captain Rust. "Is that all you're going to ask me?"

Captain Rust was also frustrated but did not see the value in further questioning, so he said, "No more questions, Your Honor."

Judge Altgelt instructed, "Call your next witness, Counsel."

Prosecutor Walker said, "The State calls Julius Voelcker."

The doors opened to the courtroom, and Julius walked in, with all eyes on him. He walked in like a man on a mission, showing a slight bit of sadness of a father who lost his lovely child. He was going to face the man he had no doubt murdered his daughter.

The judge said, "Mr. Voelcker, raise your right hand and place your left on the Bible. Do you solemnly swear to tell the truth, the whole truth, and nothing but the truth, so help you God?"

Mr. Voelcker replied, "I do, Your Honor."

Prosecutor Walker stood up and said, "Mr. Voelcker, can you introduce yourself to the jury?"

Mr. Voelcker said, "I am a simple farmer and owner of a drugstore in town." He paused for a moment, looked at Mr. Faust, and said, "I am also the proud father of Emily Voelcker."

Prosecutor Walker looked down and then at Mr. Voelcker and asked, "Mr. Voelcker, I am going to have to ask you a series of questions that are very sensitive about the night your daughter was murdered."

Mr. Voelcker said, "I am here to speak for my daughter, and I knew this day was coming, so go ahead, sir."

"On the night of your daughter's murder, can you tell us how you discovered your daughter was murdered."

Mr. Voelcker took a breath and said, "My wife and I were sound asleep, and I heard a scream. My son pounded on the door, screaming. I checked in Emma's room. Mrs. Faust was bleeding from her head, and my … my daughter was lifeless and full of blood. My wife was at the doorway, and she screamed. My son yelled, 'Papa, Papa, the man ran.' I could not figure why Mrs. Faust's dogs were not barking, but I heard a horse in the dark at full gallop leaving toward town. It was the worst night of my life."

The men on the jury studied Mr. Voelcker. All were proud, strong men, but all were in thought about perhaps a young daughter, niece, or neighbor that they could imagine as young Emma and themselves at the witness stand. Testifying was not an easy task for any person who had their child murdered.

"Did you see the man who entered your home and unleashed such violence?"

Mr. Voelcker replied, "I did not see the man, but I know it had to be the devil. Only he could do such a terrible thing."

Prosecutor Walker asked, "What was Mrs. Faust doing in your child's bedroom?"

"Mrs. Faust is a friend of my wife. She would stay in Emma's room, and Emma would sleep in the living room when Mr. Faust worked late; she did not want to stay home alone. They would often share the room, so Emma did not have to sleep in the living room."

"Did you know Mr. William Faust, and do you see him in the courtroom?"

"Yes, he is sitting across from me. Yes, he was a friend for over five years; I was a witness at their wedding."

Prosecutor Walker asked, "Do you think that man, Mr. Faust, killed your daughter?"

Mr. Voelcker looked at Mr. Faust and said, "I have no direct knowledge or reason why, but I have cooperated with this investigation and believe all the evidence and witnesses are accurate."

"Thank you, Mr. Voelcker. I have no more questions."

Judge Altgelt looked at the Defense and said, "Your witness, Counsel."

Captain Rust stood. "Mr. Voelcker, I do have to ask you some questions as you said Mr. Faust was a good friend and deserves a fair trial and defense, especially if you honored him as a witness at his wedding."

Mr. Voelcker said, "I understand."

Captain Rust continued, "I want to clarify for the jury that at no time did you see Mr. Faust in your home the night of the murder, nor did you see him leaving your home?"

Mr. Voelcker said, "No, I did not see him at the home when the murder took place."

Captain Rust then abruptly said, "I have no more questions, and I am sorry for your loss, Mr. Voelcker."

Judge Altgelt said, "Mr. Voelcker, you may step down. Counsel, call your next witness."

Prosecutor Walker said, "The State calls Mrs. Voelcker."

Mrs. Voelcker entered the courtroom. Young Emil and her husband, Julius Voelcker, escorted her arm in arm, one on each side, and then took their seats.

Judge Altgelt said, "Can you hold up your right hand and place your left hand on the Bible? Do you swear to tell the truth, the whole truth, and nothing but the truth, so help you God?"

"I do, sir."

Prosecutor Walker said, "I thank you for coming in, Mrs. Voelcker. I have a few questions and will make this as short as possible."

Mrs. Voelcker nodded her head in compliance.

"Can you introduce yourself to the jury?" the prosecutor asked.

Mrs. Voelcker replied, "I am Louisa Voelcker, mother of Emma Voelcker and wife of Julius Voelcker."

Prosecutor Walker said, "I know this is hard, but can you tell us about the events of your daughter's murder."

Mrs. Voelcker looked at Faust and was quiet for a moment. She then looked at her son and husband in the first row of seats. Speaking slowly, she said, "I will never forget the night I heard Mrs. Faust scream. Emma was hit so hard she did not have a chance to scream. Mrs. Faust's dogs were panting, but none barked, which was strange since they bark at anyone close to Mrs. Faust. Julius sprang up as we heard Emil push our door open in terror."

Mrs. Voelcker looked as if she were trying to regain her composure. She wiped tears from her eyes and started to speak again in a more stern tone, saying, "I saw my daughter, I could not make her face out; I was in a panic. I had to leave the room; she was covered in blood and lifeless. Julius took over, I was more in the way."

Prosecutor Walker stared directly at the Defense and said, "Ma'am, thank you for your testimony. I will not have you relive this night again. I am sure the defense would agree your beautiful angel was murdered. I do need to ask you about your accounts of the person suspected of the crime. Mrs. Voelcker, you mentioned Mrs. Faust's two small dogs were with her. Do they normally bark at strangers?"

Mrs. Voelcker answered, "All the time. They barked at us

until they got to know us, and they would occasionally still bark at my husband."

Prosecutor Walker asked, "Do the dogs bark at Mr. Faust?"

Mrs. Voelcker quickly said, "No, I have never seen them bark at Mr. Faust. The dogs are very obedient to him."

Captain Rust blurted, "Your Honor, I object. This sounds like the State is insinuating that dogs are being used to identify my client as the murderer. What is next? Are we going to let the horses identify my client?"

Judge Altgelt looked annoyed, and Prosecutor Walker said, "Your Honor, we have a witness who was at the scene of a crime, and describing important observations made at the time the crime was committed and using the horses does not sound like a bad idea."

Captain Rust shouted, "Your Honor, this is ridiculous. This man is on trial for his life, and the State is putting on circumstantial evidence because there is no real evidence."

Judge Altgelt calmly said, "I will allow the testimony, but we will not be getting into animal behavior unless it pertains to the merits of this case. State, you may continue."

Prosecutor Walker pointed at Mr. Faust and said, "By the way, do you know that man?"

Mrs. Voelcker straightened her posture and clearly said, "Yes, I do."

Prosecutor Walker asked, "Mrs. Voelcker, can you explain to me how long you have known this man?"

"Mr. Faust was a friend to the family, a very good friend to my husband. We have known him and his wife for over five years."

Prosecutor Walker asked, "Was there any jewelry or valuables in the room where your daughter was murdered?"

Mrs. Voelcker answered, "There was jewelry laid out on

the drawers by the lamp. The murderer could have simply taken those without hurting anyone."

Prosecutor Walker looked at the jury and to the defense and asked Mrs. Voelcker, "Do you think Mr. Faust killed your daughter?"

Captain Rust jumped up and said, "Your Honor, this question has been asked and answered. She already testified she did not see my client murder her daughter."

Prosecutor Walker blurted back, "Your Honor, the testimony does not end after the crime. The witness did have contact with Mr. Faust well after the crime was committed, which makes it necessary for the jurors to hear all the facts of this horrendous murder."

Judge Altgelt looked at both men and sternly said, "Approach the bench, gentlemen."

Prosecutor Walker and Captain Rust eyed each other in cold silence as they walked to the judge's bench.

Judge Altgelt looked sharply at the counselors as he spoke and said, "Now remember this, this is my courtroom, and we are going to proceed on this most serious matter professionally. None of this will get personal."

Judge Altgelt pointed to Prosecutor Walker and said, "You are representing the State and the victims."

Judge Altgelt pointed to Captain Rust and said, "You, sir, are representing your client. Gentlemen, do I make myself clear? You are not representing yourselves. You all may proceed with respect to my bench."

Both counselors returned to their tables, this time not looking at each other. They both wanted to contest the judge's words, but both knew it was not a wise idea to disagree with a judge who was a stickler for the rules.

Judge Altgelt said, "To answer your objection, Captain Rust, it is overruled. I will allow it."

Prosecutor Walker said, "I apologize for the delay, but, Mrs. Voelcker, out of respect I will rephrase my question to make things clearer for the jurors' understanding. Mrs. Voelcker, did you have contact with Mr. Faust after the murder of your precious daughter?"

Mrs. Voelcker answered, "Mr. Faust avoided me after the murder, but I did go see Mrs. Faust, and he was there by her side at their home. He would not let me talk to her by myself. I asked him three questions about the murder and attack on his wife."

Prosecutor Walker asked, "What were those questions?"

Mrs. Voelcker responded, "I asked him why he never gave his condolences to myself or my husband, I asked why he was not assisting in the search for my daughter's murderer, and why did the dogs not bark at an intruder near Mrs. Faust."

"How did Mr. Faust respond to your questioning?"

Mrs. Voelcker said, "He never answered me fully. He did say he was going to search for his wife's attacker, but he fled the law instead."

The jury members were eagerly listening to every word, and the courtroom audience muttered in reaction to Mrs. Voelcker's words.

The judge raised his voice and said, "There will be order in this courtroom. If you cannot be quiet, I will have the bailiffs escort you out."

Prosecutor Walker knew that Mrs. Voelcker was highly respected in the city and her word was gold. He did realize that there was only one person who identified Mr. Faust in the area of the crime scene, and he had to stick to the evidence. Mrs. Voelcker or any of the Voelcker family could have easily said that they saw Faust in the home, but they could not honestly say that. Even with the facts and the city gossip, about Faust being the murderer, the family stuck to their honor. Even though in their hearts they knew that Faust was the killer, they spoke the truth, and Prosecutor Walker had to make sure there were no doubts and all his witnesses spoke the truth.

Prosecutor Walker looked to the judge and said, "No more questions, Your Honor."

The judge looked at Captain Rust and asked, "Do you wish to examine the witness?"

Captain Rust was hesitant; he knew he did not get a change of venue granted and that the entire town knew of the case. He knew he had to show his sympathy in front of the jurors or from this point on he would lose the jury. He looked at the jury, and all eyes were on him. He still had their attention and needed to get his point across and at the same time show his sympathy to the mother of an innocent daughter who was brutally murdered. His strategy was to encourage the jurors to listen and balance his argument and weigh the evidence, which was highly circumstantial from his perspective.

Captain Rust looked at Mrs. Voelcker and calmly said, "Again, I am deeply sorry for the loss of your angel. I only have one question. As you were asked previously, did you see my client, Mr. William Faust, commit the murder or assault Mrs. Helen Faust in your home on that dreadful night?"

Mrs. Voelcker said, "No, I did not."

Captain Rust said somberly, "No more questions, Your Honor."

The judge then asked Prosecutor Walker, "Any more questions from the State?"

"No, Your Honor, no further questions."

The judge said, "Mrs. Voelcker, you may step down."

Prosecutor Walker immediately stood up and escorted Mrs. Voelcker off the stand to her awaiting family members.

"That will be all for today, ladies and gentlemen," the judge said. "We will reconvene at eight thirty in the morning."

The bailiff yelled, "All rise," and the jury was escorted under guard by deputies to the hotel across the courthouse for the night.

Captain Rust said to Mr. Faust, "I will come visit you tonight."

The courtroom emptied out as the crowd slowly shuffled out the door. Three deputies stood guard over Faust, and when one of the deputies cleared the hallway, courtroom, and walkways, he was escorted back to the town jail, which needed repair. Faust was quiet and smoked a cigar in his jail cell. The deputies brought him his meal, but he did not eat.

Captain Rust came in about an hour later and noticed his client sitting on his bunk with his hands on his head, looking down toward the floor.

Captain Rust said, "Evening, William. I brought you some biscuits from the bakery."

Mr. Faust spoke while looking at the ground. "It seems like nobody is going to believe me no matter what you say; their minds are made up. You know, I have seen people hang; they put you up in the square in front of everyone. Women and children are there. I have seen the law hang plenty with sometimes just an accusation. At least I know my wife won't be able to see me hang if they take me out in a few days and hang me."

Captain Rust said, "That is why it is important we talk, William. Nobody saw you at the crime scene, William, and from what you're telling me, you were not there. I believe if you knew these folks pretty well, somebody would have recognized you."

Mr. Faust said, "You are right. Nobody has said they saw me there, and nobody was able to because it was not me in their home that night."

Captain Rust said, "The cross-examinations are going to

get a lot tougher; can we still count on your wife to vouch for you?"

Mr. Faust said, "I have no doubts, but her family has always hated me."

Captain Rust said, "Well, that is understandable. I am still not sure if my in-laws love me to this day after fifteen years of marriage."

Captain Rust then said, "I will see you in the courtroom in the morning." Before leaving, he glanced around the place and said, "It looks like the jail is falling apart."

Mr. Faust said, "Good night. I hope tomorrow is a better day."

Captain Rust looked to the deputy and said, "Deputy, I am done."

The deputy came and opened the cell for Captain Rust, and he left the small five-cell jail.

• •

Isom Taylor had left the courtroom and met his daughter and wife before departing the city. He and his family noticed uncomfortable stares by some town members, but there were other town members who nodded to the family with respect.

His wife said, "I need to get some things in the general store. We will just be a minute."

Isom walked a little way, and in between the general store and pharmacy, two men suddenly pulled him into the alley between the buildings. They had covered their faces with bandanas and said, "You better think twice about opening your mouth, boy. We know everything about you." They fired a shot in the air, and one of the men punched him in the stomach, causing Isom to fall to the ground.

Ada, Isom's daughter, and his wife, Hilda, ran to the commotion and found Isom on the ground.

Hilda screamed, "Are you shot?"

Isom said, "No, they punched me in the stomach and ran off."

The sheriff and a deputy were in their offices and heard the shot. They both arrived with weapons drawn and asked, "Isom, are you okay?"

Isom said, "Yes, sir. They hit me with a fist. I was not shot, sir."

Sheriff Saur told his deputies, "Search the area, and Isom, stay at the hotel, where I have guards posted for the jury. Don't talk to the jury, but you and your family will be safe there."

Isom looked at his wife and daughter, both distraught over the ordeal.

Isom looked at his daughter and said, "Sir, let me stand up. I will stay here in town, and not a thing will stop me from testifying for that poor child."

Sheriff Saur said, "Isom, thank you; the city needs you. You will probably be testifying tomorrow or the day after for sure."

The sheriff personally escorted Isom and his family to the hotel and advised the deputy to watch for anything suspicious.

CHAPTER 11

DAY TWO OF THE FAUST TRIAL

Isom prepared himself and his family for court and walked across the square to the courthouse. The courtroom was already packed, and folks were already standing due to no available seating. The judge was already on the bench, speaking with Prosecutor Walker and Captain Rust. Faust was sitting at the defense table, looking calm but tired.

The judge motioned to the bailiff to bring in the jury, and the bailiff went across the street to summon the jurors.

The jurors entered the courtroom, and the bailiff bellowed, "All rise for the jury!"

Once the jury was seated, the judge advised all in the courtroom to be seated.

Judge Altgelt looked toward Prosecutor Walker and said, "You may call your next witness."

Prosecutor Walker stood up and said, "The State calls Dr. Lehde."

Dr. Lehde entered the courtroom, and the judge swore him in. He was seated at the witness stand.

Prosecutor Walker asked, "Doctor, can you state your full name for the jury and give a brief summary of your expertise?"

Dr. Lehde responded, "My name is Dr. Mark Lehde. I have been practicing medicine for over thirty years."

Prosecutor Walker asked, "Doctor, can you tell us what happened the night young Emma Voelcker was murdered and Mrs. Faust was attacked?"

Dr. Lehde said, "I responded to the home of the Voelckers and saw that young Emma Voelcker had one large wound to the left side of her head near the ear. This was a blow that caused a lot of damage, fracturing her skull and forcing bone fragments into her brain. Mrs. Faust had a wound above her eye that sliced through her eyelids and cut her hair. Emma was already dead, and I did not think Mrs. Faust was going to make it but she did."

Prosecutor Walker walked over to the bailiff's desk and grabbed an ax. He showed the ax to the Defense and the judge and said, "I would like to present this ax as exhibit A." He then walked over to Dr. Lehde and asked, "Doctor, is this the same ax that you examined after the murder?"

Dr. Lehde examined the ax and said, "Yes, it is."

"What were the results of the examination?"

"I examined the ax under a microscope and found blood and bone fragments on the blade. I could not determine if the initials were WF or a faded WE."

Prosecutor Walker then asked, "Doctor, in your expert opinion, could this ax inflict the damage that Emma Voelcker and Helen Faust suffered on the day of the attack?"

Dr. Lehde looked at the ax for a moment and replied, "The ax is sharp enough to cause the damage inflicted to the two victims, and the wounds are consistent lengths compared to the length of the blade."

Prosecutor Walker said, "Your Honor, we have no more questions."

Judge Altgelt said, "Defense, your witness."

Captain Rust began, "Dr. Lehde, thank you for your testimony. I have one question. Could the wounds inflicted on Mrs. Faust and Emma have been caused by a smaller ax or hatchet?"

Dr. Lehde said, "It is possible. There are other factors, such as the length of the handle and the strength of the person forcing the swing of the weapon."

Captain Rust said, "So it is possible that the wounds inflicted on the two victims could have been caused by a smaller hatchet or ax?"

Dr. Lehde responded, "Yes, sir ... that is also a possibility; it is a common ax."

Captain Rust stared at Prosecutor Walker, expecting a re-cross, and said, "Thank you. Your Honor, no more questions."

Judge Altgelt looked at the prosecutor and said, "If you all are through, this witness may step down, and call your next witness."

Prosecutor Walker wrote some notes and stood up. "Your Honor, the State calls Isom Taylor."

The doors to the courtroom opened, and Isom Taylor walked toward the witness stand. He did not look at anyone in the courtroom; he was focused on what he had to do. All eyes were on Isom Taylor, and the courtroom was silent except for Isom's footsteps. He stopped at the judge's bench and stood at attention, waiting for the judge to direct him.

Judge Altgelt broke the silence and said, "Mr. Taylor, raise your right hand."

Isom raised his right hand and placed his left on the Holy Bible on the bench. The judge asked, "Do you swear to tell the truth, the whole truth, and nothing but the truth, so help you God?"

Isom Taylor answered, "Yes, Your Honor, I do."

Prosecutor Walker said, "Good morning, Mr. Taylor. Can you state your full name and your living?"

Isom Taylor said, "My full name is Isom Taylor, and I have been a freeman for over ten years. I work as a hand on farms and ranches to earn my living."

Prosecutor Walker asked, "Where were you during the early morning hours of July 23, 1874?"

Isom Taylor responded, "I was fishing for catfish on the Guadalupe River in between New Braunfels and Seguin, just off the main path."

Prosecutor Walker asked, "Did you run into anyone while you were fishing that night?"

Isom Taylor answered, "Yes, I did. I ran into Mr. William Faust."

Prosecutor Walker asked, "Can you point to that man in the courtroom you are referring to as Mr. Faust and tell us how you know Mr. Faust?"

Isom Taylor pointed to Faust, who sharply stared at Isom. The black man looked at Faust directly in the eyes, and he did not look down or away.

Isom put his finger down and looked directly at Faust as he spoke. "I have known Mr. Faust for a few years; he is the only pharmacist I go to for medicine."

Prosecutor Walker said, "Please explain in full detail your encounter with Mr. Faust that night and the time you think it was."

Isom Taylor said, "Well, I was by myself fishing well after midnight. I heard a rider approaching from New Braunfels headed toward Seguin, which sounded like a full gallop. I could hear the rider getting closer, and then I heard the horse slow down. I heard a loud splash in the water. I put my pole down and wanted to make sure nobody was thrown off the horse into the river. I noticed Mr. Faust on a painted horse that I recognized from the inn in Seguin. It looked exactly like the one Mr. Johnson owned in Seguin at the Stagecoach Inn. I said to Mr. Faust, 'Good evening, sir. It's me, Isom Taylor.' I wanted to make sure he knew I was no robber or something like that. He did not look at me; he looked away and started to ride heavy again toward Seguin."

Prosecutor Walker asked, "What makes you sure that it was Mr. Faust?"

Isom Taylor said, "As I said before, I had seen him before at the pharmacy, and it was full moon, he did not have his hat on, and I could see his bald head. I also could see the painted horse pattern on the horse he was riding. I used to help my friend George, who works at the inn in Seguin, saddle the horses when he hurt his foot."

Prosecutor Walker said, "Let the record reflect that a witness has identified Mr. William Faust and has testified that he was fleeing from the direction of the murder right after it took place." Then he finished by saying, "I have no more questions of this witness."

Judge Altgelt looked at the Defense and said, "You may proceed."

Captain Rust walked directly to Isom Taylor and stood closer to him than the other witnesses who had previously testified.

"Mr. Taylor, would you say you are an honest man?"

Isom Taylor looked to Prosecutor Walker, and Walker said, "Your Honor, this man has taken an oath and swore to testify truthfully under that oath. This is out of line."

Captain Rust countered, "Your Honor, this is establishing

credibility of the witness, and I will elaborate further in my questioning."

Judge Altgelt said, "I am going to allow it."

Captain Rust asked, "Mr. Taylor, when did you learn of the Voelcker murders?"

Isom Taylor responded, "I learned the next evening that Mrs. Faust was attacked and the Voelcker child was killed."

"Did you tell anyone of this encounter with Mr. Faust the night of the murders?"

Isom Taylor replied, "I told my daughter, and I told Sheriff Saur a few days later."

Captain Rust then asked, "Why did you not report this incident sooner?"

Isom Taylor said, "For the exact reason you are asking me this question. I thought nobody would believe me because I am a former slave who could not testify or sit on a jury."

Captain Rust had one hand on his hip, paused for a moment, and then spoke in a condescending tone. "So, who else can testify your whereabouts on that night and corroborate that you saw Mr. Faust?"

Isom Taylor responded, "My daughter can verify my story, sir."

Captain Rust continued to speak in a louder, condescending tone toward Isom and asked, "Are you aware that Mr. Faust is a druggist, a respectable profession, and he is respected by many prominent members in the Seguin community?"

Isom Taylor responded, "Sir, I have no ill will against Mr. Faust. I am simply testifying to what I witnessed."

Captain Rust was surprised at Isom's answer, realizing he was failing to intimidate him. Captain Rust paused as if he was waiting to launch his attack, but puzzlingly, he only repeated a previous question. "Mr. Taylor, for the record, do you consider yourself an honest man?"

Prosecutor Walker nearly stood up to object, but Isom answered very quickly, "Yes, sir, that is why I am here."

Captain Rust looked at the judge and smirked at Prosecutor Walker before saying, "No more questions, Your Honor."

The judge looked at Prosecutor Walker and asked, "Does the State wish to reexamine this witness?"

"No, Your Honor."

Judge Altgelt said, "Witness, you may step down, and you are subject to being recalled."

Captain Rust stood up and said, "Your Honor, may I approach the bench?"

Judge Altgelt nodded his head in approval, and Prosecutor Walker approached the bench along with his adversary.

Captain Rust asked, "Judge, Isom Taylor testified on crucial testimony, and I have witnesses that discredit his testimony. I strongly feel that it brings an issue of doubt in Isom Taylor's testimony, and the jury needs to hear the testimony to decide the outcome of this case."

Prosecutor Walker said, "Isom Taylor is not on trial here. He has sworn to the testimony he provided, and the weight of the evidence has been previously evaluated in the preliminary hearing."

Judge Altgelt paused for a moment and then ruled, "I will allow the testimony as long as the testimony is connected to this particular matter."

Judge Altgelt paused again and said, "This case is a test not only for Comal County and the state of Texas regarding our nation's most bloody battle; we will keep any issues in the courtrooms where they belong and not on the battlefields. I do not want this issue to be the focus of the trial; the murder of a child is the issue."

Prosecutor Walker said, "Very well. We are prepared."

Captain Rust nodded in approval and said, "Then let us begin."

Prosecutor Walker asked, "Judge, the State would like to call its next witness, Ada Martinez."

Young Ada Martinez was the stepdaughter of Isom Taylor. She looked a bit nervous but held her composure. Judge Altgelt swore Ada Martinez in, and Prosecutor Walker approached his witness to begin his examination.

Prosecutor Walker asked, "Can you introduce yourself to the jury?"

Ada Martinez responded, "I am Ada Martinez. I am seventeen years old and from Seguin, Texas."

"Do you recall what your father, Isom Taylor, told you about William Faust around July 23, 1874?"

Ada Martinez answered, "My father told me he had seen Mr. Faust the night of the murder, but he did not tell me until late that evening. He did not think much about it until he heard the news, I told him he should talk to the sheriff."

Prosecutor Walker asked, "Are you sure it was the evening of July 23?"

The young lady replied, "Yes, sir, I checked on the calendar to make sure."

Prosecutor Walker asked, "Is there anything you recall that Isom Taylor told you about the Faust murders, and did your father mention any quarrels with him?"

Ada Martinez replied, "No, sir, that is all, and he had no quarrels he mentioned with Mr. Faust."

The prosecutor walked away and said, "Your Honor, I have no more questions."

Judge Altgelt looked at Captain Rust. "Counsel, your witness."

Captain Rust had some written words on some papers and asked the judge, "Can I approach the witness?"

The judge allowed it, and Captain Rust approached young Ada Martinez and asked, "Ada Martinez, are you able to read and write?"

Ada Martinez said, "Yes, I have had schooling."

Captain Rust said, "Very well. Can you read to the jury these three words on this piece of paper?"

She looked at the words and paused.

Captain Rust blurted, "Well, we are all waiting for you. Go ahead."

Ada Martinez then responded, "January, March, and June."

Captain Rust yanked the paper from her hand and said, "Did your father in any way persuade you to say anything today about the murders?"

Ada Martinez responded, "Yes, he told me to tell the truth."

Captain Rust sharply retorted, "So, you are telling me truthfully that you are saying your father, Isom Taylor, only told you and not your mother?"

"Yes, sir. I saw him first that evening, and I told him Mother would get worried."

Captain Rust looked to the judge and said, "I have no more use for this witness."

Judge Altgelt looked at Ada and said, "You may step down."

Captain Rust then said, "Your Honor, if I may call my next witness, Joseph Zorn."

"You may proceed," said the judge, and then he swore in Joseph Zorn.

Captain Rust began, "As you know, Mr. Zorn, this case is of the utmost importance, and I am asking you to tell this jury the events you remember on July 22 regarding William Faust."

Joseph Zorn replied, "Well, I really have no idea why I

am here, but I will tell you what I know. I saw Mr. Faust on the day before in Seguin, and he was wearing a light-colored shirt and a dark coat. The next morning, I saw him again in Seguin; he was wearing the same thing, and two marshals were talking to him."

Captain Rust asked, "Do you know Isom Taylor?"

The man responded sharply, "Yes, I do and would not believe a word he said, even under oath."

Captain Rust smiled. "Your Honor, I have no more questions."

Prosecutor Walker stood up and said, "Your Honor, I just have one question for this witness."

"You may proceed."

"Mr. Zorn," Walker said sternly, "can you tell the jury why you would not believe a word Mr. Isom Taylor said?"

Joseph Zorn said, "Well, because I just know such things."

Prosecutor Walker pressed him. "Well, if we all simply knew such things, there would be no need to have a trial here, but we are all here today for a reason: young Emma Voelcker. Mr. Zorn, please give an example why you do not believe Isom Taylor's testimony."

Joseph Zorn began fidgeting in his seat and then shouted, "Well, you know, I know this through good friends and town gossip."

Prosecutor Walker looked at Joseph Zorn and said, "Well, gentlemen of the jury, we certainly can't hold weight on gossip or hearsay in a court of law. No more questions, Your Honor."

Judge Altgelt turned to Mr. Zorn and said, "You may step down. Call your next witness."

Captain Rust stood up. "Your Honor, the Defense calls Roland Johnston."

Judge Altgelt swore the witness in and advised him to be seated on the witness stand.

Captain Rust asked, "Mr. Johnston, can you state your full name and your occupation for the jury?"

Roland Johnston said, "I am the owner of the Stagecoach Inn, where Faust stayed on the night the murders were committed. I did not know about the murders for a while until I was questioned by deputies. On the night in question of the murders, Faust stayed in room three of the inn and went to bed about nine forty-five. I personally spoke to him when he checked in, and we talked for a bit. I opened the door to room three and advised him to have a good night. I caught up on some paperwork for the next day and locked up the inn at ten thirty and went to bed. I did not hear or see Mr. Faust leave the room and would have heard if he did. I also own the horse that Isom Taylor claimed he saw Mr. Faust riding the night of the murders. The horse was in the pen and looked rested. I saw no indication that it had been ridden hard at night. I would have noticed if the horse was taken at night; it would have caused a stir with the other horses and guests. This horse is not easy to catch and saddle during the day, and I doubt anyone could accomplish this in the dark."

Captain Rust said, "Well, thank you, Mr. Johnston, for giving the jury such fine detail of the accounts." He chuckled and said, "Your Honor, I have no more questions."

Prosecutor Walker walked to the witness and said, "Your Honor, I have some questions for this witness."

Judge Altgelt said, "Proceed."

"Just to be clear, Mr. Johnston," the prosecutor said, "Mr. Faust was at your inn when he has a home in Seguin. Did he say why he was staying at the inn?"

Mr. Roland Johnston was quiet for a moment before finally replying, "Mr. Faust was known to stay as a patron of the inn salon."

"Mr. Johnston, your inn is for usually for stagecoach guests who stop passing through, isn't it?"

"Yes, sir, it is."

Prosecutor Walker asked, "It is kind of strange that Mr. Faust made it a point for you to see him that night and not stay at home about two miles away, how often does Faust stay?"

Mr. Roland Johnston said, "I see your point, but I usually do not ask questions as to why a guest is staying at my inn, Faust frequents the saloon but rarely stays the entire night."

Prosecutor Walker asked, "Mr. Johnston, would you also say that even though you did not see Mr. Faust leave, would it still be possible for him to leave and be back without you knowing if that were his plan?"

Mr. Roland Johnston looked real uneasy and did not know what to say for a moment. Finally he said, "Well, I guess if that would be someone's intentions. I would never stop anyone from leaving unless I had not been paid for the stay, and he did pay me in advance."

Prosecutor Walker turned to the judge and said, "Your Honor, I have no more questions."

Judge Altgelt said, "Very well; call your next witness."

Prosecutor Walker said, "Judge, the State calls George Johnston."

George Johnston was an average-size black male except for a toned physique from working with his hands his entire life.

Judge Altgelt swore him in, and he sat at the witness stand ready to respond.

Prosecutor Walker asked, "Mr. George Johnston, can you tell us what you do for a living?"

George Johnston said, "I am a former slave who has worked for my former master, Mr. Roland Johnston, since the end of the war. I handle the guests' horses and Mr. Johnston's horses. I also train and keep up with the pens."

Prosecutor Walker asked, "Mr. Johnston, do you take care of a painted horse at the inn in Seguin that is owned by Roland Johnston?"

George Johnston replied, "Yes, sir. That is one of the younger horses, and it is known to be fast, but I disagree with Roland Johnston; anyone could corral and saddle that horse. The horse loves to be ridden and will saddle up quickly."

The prosecutor next asked, "Mr. George Johnston, since you take care of the horses at the inn, has the painted pony made a round trip from Seguin in a time frame of three to four hours?"

George Johnston answered, "Yes, sir. That horse could make that trip in a little under three hours. No doubt everyone who has stayed at the inn knows that is our top horse, Mr. Faust has ridden it several times."

Prosecutor Walker looked at Judge Altgelt and said, "No more questions, Your Honor."

Judge Altgelt looked at Captain Rust and said, "Very well then, your witness."

Captain Rust approached George Johnston and said, "I just have a few questions, Mr. Johnston. On the night of the murder, did you see Mr. Faust take the horse and return it?"

George Johnston replied, "Well, no, sir. I just said it was possible."

Captain Rust sharply responded, "Sir, that is not what I asked you. I did not ask you what is possible. I asked you what you saw. Now answer the question. Did you see that man"—he pointed at Mr. Faust—"take a horse from the pen at your inn during the middle of the night on the same night as the murder?"

George Johnston answered, "No, I did not see Mr. Faust take the horse on the night of the murder."

Captain Rust looked at Prosecutor Walker and to the judge and said, "I have no more questions, Your Honor."

Prosecutor Walker calmly shook his head, and Judge Altgelt dismissed George Johnston from the witness stand.

Captain Rust said, "Your Honor, I call my next witness, Robert Carpenter."

Robert Carpenter was a neighbor of Faust who made a simple but hard living farming off his property in Seguin.

Judge Altgelt swore Robert Carpenter as a witness, and he was seated in the witness stand.

Captain Rust asked, "Mr. Carpenter, can you state your full name and occupation for the jury?"

Robert Carpenter was extremely disgruntled and said, "I do not know why I am here, but my name is Robert Carpenter, and I am a simple farmer."

Captain Rust asked, "Can you explain your dealings with Isom Taylor?"

Robert Carpenter said, "Yes. He has done some work on the farm for me and tried to say I owed him more than what I paid him. He is a damn liar."

Captain Rust asked, "Would you believe his testimony, even though he was sworn in by Judge Altgelt to tell the truth here for this *murder* trial?"

Robert Carpenter responded angrily, "No, I would not believe Isom Taylor."

Captain Rust said, "Thank you, sir. I have no more questions."

Prosecutor Walker stood up. "I have a few questions. Mr. Carpenter. What was the dispute about with Isom Taylor?"

Robert Carpenter said, "Isom Taylor did not finish the job, so I did not pay him for the job."

Prosecutor Walker asked, "Well, did you settle the dispute?"

Robert Carpenter crossed his arms and said, "We did. I paid him for my name's sake."

The prosecutor looked at the judge and said, "No more questions."

The judge ordered Robert Carpenter off the stand.

Prosecutor Walker and Captain Rust stood up at the same time, and Judge Altgelt scolded both counselors and said, "Now look, this trial is not about Isom Taylor. It is about the murder of young Emma Voelcker. I will only allow one more witness from each side, and then we are moving on to testimony other than Isom Taylor."

Judge Altgelt looked at both counselors anticipating a rebuttal and said, "Prosecutor Walker, call your next witness."

Prosecutor Walker said, "I call Sheriff John Gordon of Guadalupe County."

Sheriff John Gordon walked in with a poker face without looking at anyone. He stopped and raised his right hand in front of the judge's bench. Judge Altgelt swore him in as a witness, and Sheriff Gordon sat down on the witness chair.

Prosecutor Walker asked, "Sheriff Gordon, can you identify yourself and state your occupation to the jury?"

Sheriff Gordon said, "My name is John Gordon. I have been the Guadalupe County Sheriff for the past fifteen years."

"Do you know Isom Taylor, and would you believe his testimony under oath?"

Sheriff Gordon said, "I have absolutely no reason to doubt Mr. Taylor's testimony. I have never had any dealings with him in my time as sheriff in Guadalupe County."

"Thank you, Sheriff Gordon, I have no more questions."

Judge Altgelt turned to Captain Rust and asked, "Do you wish to examine this witness?"

Captain Rust answered, "No, Your Honor. I will call my next witness, Judge Edward White."

Prosecutor Walker knew that Judge White was a witness that the defense would call but was not sure why. Judge White had previously held Faust on bond, ruling enough evidence supported probable cause.

Judge White went to the witness stand and was sworn in by Judge Altgelt.

Captain Rust said, "Judge White, please identify yourself to the jury."

Judge White said, "I am Judge Edward White, and I have been a judge for twenty-five years."

Captain Rust asked, "Judge White, did you hear the preliminary hearing on this case?"

Judge White replied, "Yes, I did."

Captain Rust asked, "Do you think that the testimony of Isom Taylor during the time of the preliminary hearing is valid?"

Judge White responded, "*No, I do not!*"

The courtroom began to chatter, which caused Judge Altgelt to yell, "Order in the court!"

Prosecutor Walker said, "Your Honor, Judge White has already made a ruling previously that has jailed Mr. Faust since he was apprehended. That testimony is a matter of record; this is not his opportunity to change his ruling by testifying in this hearing."

Judge Altgelt looked annoyed and confused, knowing that this was unusual for a judge to second-guess his own ruling under oath. Nonetheless, he said, "I will allow this."

Captain Rust asked, "Judge White, why have you changed your mind?"

Judge White said, "I have heard more testimony in this trial, and with my experience as a judge, I no longer believe Isom Taylor."

The crowd began to get upset. It was unheard of from

a judge to make a statement on his own previous ruling, contradicting himself. Judge Altgelt again demanded order in the court, and the courtroom quickly silenced.

Captain Rust smiled to Prosecutor Walker and said, "No more questions, Your Honor."

Prosecutor Walker stood up and asked, "Judge White, do you believe now that Mr. Faust should not have been jailed and should have been allowed to be free before this trial? As you well know, the sheriff had to apprehend Mr. Faust since he fled from justice."

Judge White said, "I still believe Mr. Faust should be jailed, but the weight of Isom Taylor's testimony should not be considered by the jury."

Prosecutor Walker said, "So, to be clear, you ruled in favor of jailing Mr. Faust based on the evidence presented to you, which included Mr. Taylor's testimony?"

Judge White said, "I have observed more witnesses come forward testifying against Mr. Taylor's statements under oath; this was not the case during my hearing."

Prosecutor Walker pointed and said, "Despite you being a judge, it is your judgment and statements that are now under question, and this court will determine the outcome from this point on since you cannot make up your mind. Did you also hear the testimony of the sheriff of Guadalupe County, among others, testify they would believe Mr. Taylor? Keep in mind, Sheriff Gordon has been in your court testifying on many occasions. Are you now saying you do not believe him?"

Judge White looked sharply at Prosecutor Walker. He was not accustomed to being talked to in such a way. He replied, "I believe Sheriff Gordon ... May I step down now?"

Judge Altgelt looked at both counselors, and the counselors looked at each other.

Prosecutor Walker said, "I have no more questions."

Judge Altgelt said, "It is now five o'clock, and we will continue tomorrow at eight thirty in the morning. Bailiff, escort the jury to the hotel."

CHAPTER 12

DAY THREE: FINAL DAY OF TESTIMONY IN THE TRIAL

It was a gloomy morning; the Guadalupe River would sometimes cause a mist and early fog. The courtroom was standing room only; everyone in town knew that the trial was underway and wrapping up. Judge Altgelt was on the bench, and the jury entered the courtroom. The men of the jury looked calm and alert, yet they all knew the decision was going to be a lot tougher than they had thought. The jury was going to be the judge of the facts and determine guilt or innocence. If there was a guilty verdict, the judge was going to decide the punishment.

Judge Altgelt swore in the next witness, Detective Lyons, and the detective took his seat at the witness stand.

Prosecutor Walker said, "Detective Lyons, can you introduce yourself to the jury?"

Detective Lyons answered, "My name is Detective Lyons. I am a deputy with the Comal County Sheriff's Office. I have worked there for over ten years."

"What was your role with the murder case?"

Detective Lyons replied, "My job was to locate many of the witnesses who testified here and to collect witness statements."

Prosecutor Walker asked, "Did you talk to any known criminals regarding this case?"

Detective Lyons answered, "I talked to three men known to have committed robberies who were locked up at the Bexar County Jail: Mr. Allen, Mr. Lee, and Mr. Williams."

Prosecutor Walker stood up, walked to the judge's bench, and said, "Your Honor, I have three documents I would like to present as evidence; they are the statements I will be referring to."

Judge Altgelt read through the letters and asked, "Will these three men be testifying?"

Prosecutor Walker said, "No, Your Honor, due to the security issues of the Comal County Jail, Detective Lyons helped write the statements since none could read and write."

Judge Altgelt said, "Under these circumstances, I will allow it."

Captain Rust stood up. "Your Honor, I would like the opportunity to cross-examine any witnesses against my client."

Judge Altgelt said, "We will be accepting this under Detective Lyons's statements; the witnesses are not available. Prosecutor Walker, continue."

The prosecutor handed the statements to Detective Lyons and asked, "Detective, do these documents look familiar to you; and if they do, did you generate the documents?"

Detective Lyons said, "Yes, they are my handwritten documents, I did write the statements for these men."

"Detective, can you summarize for the jury what these statements are and tell the jury your experience with criminals cooperating with the law?"

Detective Lyons said, "I located three witnesses who were

housed with Mr. Faust, and they all had heard Mr. Faust confess to the attempted murder of his wife. We corroborated information from other witnesses, beginning with these statements, that led us to a motive for the murder. This is one thing we could not figure out—why these two victims were attacked. The motivation was greed, money, and to silence a witness. It is unusual for outlaws to tell the law any information. Usually it is for one of two things: a vendetta or the lack of respect of the title of being an outlaw. In this case, the three outlaws I spoke with learned a child was murdered, and Mr. Faust gained no respect from the trio as an outlaw when he tried to talk with his bunkmates on how he would beat this case. Faust assumed the three outlaws would respect him since he was an outlaw. Faust told them he had planned to kill his wife to try to get her inheritance and then marry and murder her sister, who was getting part of a split inheritance of nearly five thousand dollars from their late father's property in Germany. Those facts were corroborated with interviews from respectable citizens such as Mr. Werner and Mrs. Rhodius, who confirmed the inheritance amounts. The outlaws were from Hondo, San Antonio, and Oklahoma; they did not know the Fausts or Rhodius, leading to the fact that the only way they would know this information was if indeed Faust told the three outlaws."

The courtroom was silent in shock, but the brother of Mrs. Faust, Edward Rhodius, blurted out, "That son of a bitch!" Most of the investigation was tight lipped, and Edward Rhodius suspected this, but no proof had been divulged to the public until now.

This time Judge Altgelt grew angry. He slammed his gavel and said, "Order in my court. If you cannot conduct yourself in an orderly way, then remove yourselves now. Next time you will be removed involuntarily."

Prosecutor Walker asked, "How did you collect the statements of the prisoners?"

Detective Lyons answered, "I took these statements you showed me from the three men. I also spoke with Joseph Werner about the money and documents that came from Germany. I learned that Mr. Faust immediately pursued Helen Rhodius when he learned about the money. They were married shortly after. We learned that Mr. Faust had a gambling debt and frequented the Stagecoach Inn to tend to prostitutes."

Prosecutor Walker passed the statements to the jurors, who looked at the documents one by one. When they finished, he said, "Your Honor, I have no more questions."

Judge Altgelt said, "Defense, your witness."

Captain Rust stood up and looked sharply at Detective Lyons. "Detective, have you always gone to known criminals to make your cases in a court of law?"

Detective Lyons replied, "From time to time, I have."

Captain Rust said, "Do you expect me to believe or anyone in this courtroom to believe that you gained a confession from known criminals against my client for a statement that you wrote?"

Detective Lyons said, "I am thorough, sir. I used these statements for the investigation. There had been no motive established, and through these statements, I was able to find more reliable evidence that led to a motive for the murder, which was money and greed."

Captain Rust said, "This appears to be a sign of desperation and a ridiculous ploy to find a motive because there was not a motive for my client to commit any murder. He had an honest profession, and money was not an issue."

Detective Lyons responded, "With greed there is always an issue with money, and again, the sheriff's office was very thorough. Robbery was not a motive; revenge on the Voelckers

117

was not a motive either, and with the evidence in hand, Mrs. Faust was clearly the intended target."

Captain Rust said, "Your Honor, again I must protest these documents and the testimony of Detective Lyons. My client should be given the opportunity to confront any witnesses against him."

Judge Altgelt said, "Denied, sir. Any more questions?"

Captain Rust said, "No, Your Honor."

Prosecutor Walker said, "I would like to call my next witness, Joseph Werner."

Judge Altgelt swore Joseph Werner in as a witness, and he was seated in the witness chair.

Prosecutor Walker said, "Can you introduce yourself to the jury, Mr. Werner?"

Mr. Werner said, "My name is Joseph Werner. I'm an attorney from Seguin, I do deeds and documents. I have known Mr. Faust for several years and was in his wedding to Helen Faust."

Prosecutor Walker asked, "Mr. Werner, can you tell us your relations with Mr. Faust?"

"Mr. Faust and I would talk now and then. My office was once next to his when he worked in Seguin. About two years ago, he walked in my office, and I was going over some documents for the Rhodius family. He asked what the documents were, and I said they were for an inheritance from Germany for the Rhodius family. I quickly put the documents away, but he was able to read a part of the documents that reflected nearly a total of ten thousand dollars, which is a lot of money. The next thing I knew, I found out William was courting Mrs. Helen Rhodius, and a few months later, he asked me to be a witness when he married her."

Prosecutor Walker asked, "Is there anything else you may be able to tell this jury about the murder of Emma Voelcker?"

Mr. Werner said, "That is the gist of it, I do not know details of the murder other than from the papers."

Prosecutor Walker asked, "Do you know Isom Taylor, and if you do, would you believe him under sworn testimony?"

Mr. Werner replied, "Yes, I know Isom Taylor and have no reason why he would lie."

Prosecutor Walker said, "Thank you, Mr. Werner. I have no more questions of this witness."

Judge Altgelt said, "Your witness, Captain Rust."

Captain Rust said, "Good morning, Mr. Werner. You mentioned you know Mr. Faust. Is that correct?"

Mr. Werner said, "Yes, I did."

"Is it true you had a confrontation with Mr. Faust sometime before the murders?"

Mr. Werner answered, "Yes. We had an issue over him not paying me for some documents I made for him. He never paid me."

Captain Rust asked, "So, it is my understanding that you want the jury to believe your testimony claiming that you were once friends and in Mr. Faust's wedding, and now that a money disagreement came up, you are testifying against him; that makes your opinion biased."

Mr. Werner was a little agitated at Captain Rust's question, and being an attorney himself, he knew he had to remain impartial in his words. He responded, "I have had no ill will toward Mr. Faust. It was he who avoided me. I do not know any more details; I am being asked what I know and giving my honest answers."

Captain Rust looked at Mr. Werner, rolled his eyes in doubt, and said, "No more questions, Your Honor. If I can call my next witness—Mrs. Helen Faust."

Mrs. Faust was blind but stood up at her seat. Mr. Voelcker and Edward Rhodius both escorted her to the witness stand.

The scars from her brutal attack were still visible around her eyes and forehead. Despite the injuries, she was still a beautiful young woman.

Mrs. Faust sat on the witness stand, and Judge Altgelt swore her in as a witness.

Captain Rust said, "Mrs. Faust, I have talked to you previously. I am Captain Rust, the man defending your husband. I am going to ask you some questions about the night you were attacked and young Emma was killed. Can you please introduce yourself to the jury; the members of the jury are seated to your left-hand side."

Mrs. Faust said, "My name is Helen Rhodius Faust. I am the wife of William Faust."

Captain Rust next asked, "As best you can, can you tell us what happened on the night you lost your eyesight and young Emma was murdered?"

Mrs. Faust paused for a moment and then began to speak. "On the night of the murder, I stayed with the Voelckers, who are dear friends of us and young Emma enjoyed my company."

Mrs. Faust paused for a moment and regained her composure.

When she began speaking again, she said, "I would usually tell young Emma a story before she went to bed, and often she fell asleep with me. We were fast asleep, and I was awoken by the bed violently shaking. I looked up and saw a dark figure above me. The dark figure swung an object that hit me near my eyes, and that was the last thing I ever saw in my life."

Captain Rust said, "Can you describe how you met your husband?"

Mrs. Faust smiled, but the smile was a sad one.

"William was an absolute gentleman. I met him about a year before this happened to me. He asked for my hand in marriage to my mother, and my mother said yes and so did I.

He has been alongside me taking care of me ever since I went blind. My husband is a druggist. I think he would have simply poisoned me if he wanted to kill me."

Captain Rust looked the jury and then to Mrs. Faust and asked, "Did you see who killed young Emma or the person who struck you that night?"

Mrs. Faust answered, "I wish I did, but I did not."

Captain Rust next asked, "Mrs. Faust, you are the only eyewitness to the murder that your husband, Mr. William Faust, is being accused of committing. Did he strike you that night, and did he kill Emma Voelcker?"

Mrs. Faust said, "William would never do such a thing. He loves me and loved Emma. The Voelckers took care of me and attended our wedding."

Captain Rust said, "Your Honor, I have no more questions of this witness."

Prosecutor Walker nodded at the judge and began his questioning.

"Mrs. Faust, I am the prosecutor for the State and representing the State and the victim. I realize that you refused to file charges against your husband, and we will not ask you to do so. I need to ask you a few more questions, though."

Mrs. Faust sharply responded, "I didn't file because he did not hit me."

Prosecutor Walker said, "I understand, Mrs. Faust; we all see things from our own points of view. The only problem is when people you know see it differently, perhaps from an outsider's perspective, but we will get to that later. I would like you to be clear when you testified that you did not see who hit you. I want to clear up for the jury that you did not see who hit you, and that means that your husband cannot be ruled out, do you agree?"

Mrs. Faust looked offended but tried to think about how she would respond.

Captain Rust stood up and said loudly, "I object. This question was asked and answered previously."

Judge Altgelt immediately said, "Overruled. She will answer the question."

Mrs. Faust said, "I do not know who it was, and the law doesn't know either; it could have been anyone."

Prosecutor Walker said, "You did not answer the question. Since you said it could be anyone, does that mean it is possible that William could have done it?"

For the first time, William Faust seemed to show interest. He cautiously looked around, anticipating his wife's answer.

Mrs. Faust said, "No, William could not have done this to me. Judge, may I step down? I do not feel well."

The judge looked at both counselors, and they both shook their heads, indicating they had no more questions. Mr. Voelcker, the gentleman that he was, escorted Mrs. Faust arm in arm to the back of the courtroom and seated her. Mr. Voelcker held no ill will knowing that Mrs. Faust was testifying for the person who killed his daughter. He retained a small bit of hope that the murderer was not William Faust, but his fatherly instincts told him otherwise.

The judge looked at the counselors and said, "Bring in your next witnesses."

Prosecutor Walker said, "The State calls Mrs. Rhodius, the mother of Helen Faust."

Mrs. Rhodius sat at the witness stand and was sworn in by Judge Altgelt.

Prosecutor Walker asked, "Mrs. Rhodius, can you introduce yourself to the jury?"

Mrs. Rhodius said, "I am the mother of Helen Faust and the mother-in-law of William Faust."

"Mrs. Walker, can you describe your relationship with Mr. Faust."

Mrs. Rhodius said, "My husband passed away a few years ago, so I am a widow, but when I first met Faust, he seemed like a hardworking man. He asked to marry my daughter, and I said yes. This behavior was short-lived; I saw his behavior change, and he became distant to the family and my daughter. He seemed to work only when he had to; he was a druggist, but often he would not be at work. He hung around that inn at the bar. People would tell me he had a girlfriend who was a prostitute there and gambled there. My relationship was good with him at first, but then it went to a distant relationship; he started to keep Helen away from the family. He would have her stay at the Voelckers so we could not visit her in our own town in Seguin. Faust also wanted to borrow money to run from the law from me, which convinced me he was hiding something."

Prosecutor Walker asked, "Did you know William to be violent with your daughter or anyone else?"

Mrs. Rhodius said, "I cannot say for sure, but my daughter was a happy person before her marriage. As you can see her now, she is not. Mr. Faust seemed to have control over her, which made her a quiet and sad person."

Prosecutor Walker then asked, "Mrs. Rhodius, as the mother of your child, would you say you know your daughter's personality?"

Mrs. Rhodius answered, "I know all my children and their personalities."

Prosecutor Walker paced back and forth and said, "Do you think your daughter was being truthful when she testified to this court?"

The crowd began muttering, and Captain Rust said, "Your Honor, I object to this line of questioning. This witness cannot tell us how another person is thinking."

Judge Altgelt responded, "I will allow it since this is the mother of this witness. You may answer, Mrs. Rhodius."

Captain Rust was infuriated with anger but sat quietly at the defense table with his arms crossed.

Mrs. Rhodius answered, "My daughter is being truthful, but she is scared, and I feel in my heart she has to know that her husband, William Faust, tried to kill her and likely Emma Voelcker."

The crowd in the courtroom became loud, chattering among one another, but quickly quieted as they knew the judge's patience was at an end.

Prosecutor Walker stated that he had no more questions. Judge Altgelt looked at Captain Rust, who shook his head no.

Prosecutor Walker stood up and said, "Your Honor, the Prosecution rests."

Captain Rust said, "Defense rests."

Judge Altgelt said, "This is a great time to break for lunch. We will hear closing arguments when we return at one thirty."

The bailiff proclaimed, "All rise!" and the courtroom emptied in a quiet chatter.

The jurors were escorted to eat their lunch under the careful watch of two of the bailiffs. The jurors were not supposed to talk about the trial until the end of the proceedings. Nonetheless, Franz spoke to all the jurors and said, "Gentlemen, I have been thinking of a way to measure all of this evidence. Let's agree on the five most important points of testimony and evidence. If the evidence tilts to three or more, then we will vote that for the outcome. We must be unanimous, or this judge will let us deliberate all week until we reach a verdict."

All the jurors nodded their heads in agreement and continued to eat their meals.

CHAPTER 13

CLOSING ARGUMENTS AND JURY DELIBERATION

The courtroom was once again full. People were waiting outside the courtroom in preparation for news or even a hanging.

Judge Altgelt said, "Defense, your closing."

Captain Rust approached the jury and began to speak. "Gentlemen, remember the words 'reasonable doubt' as I give my final statement to you all. Gentlemen of the jury, you have heard testimony from both sides. I want to remind you that it is not the responsibility of me or Mr. Faust, whom I represent, to prove he did or did not do these despicable crimes. It is the prosecution's burden, and they have not proven their case. Allow me to explain why they have not established any guilt of Mr. Faust. First, you all have heard testimony from many individuals who give no direct evidence that Mr. Faust committed these horrible crimes. We do have facts, and those are that a beautiful child has been murdered and my client's wife was brutally attacked. All that the prosecution has presented is circumstantial evidence, and they have put up a smoke screen to create eyewitnesses who are not even legitimate witnesses.

"Let me summarize what you must do and the evidence you must weigh in finding Mr. Faust guilty or not guilty. First, as you look at this packed courtroom with citizens from Seguin, New Braunfels, Austin, and San Antonio—and of course the writers of the local papers you see a lot of concerned people. This is what is called pressure for our local lawmen to make an arrest. The quickest and desperate option was to arrest William Faust, the husband of one of the victims.

"You heard very important evidence that does not convict my client; in fact, it exonerates him.

"First, we heard from the beloved Voelcker family, who were good friends with Mr. Faust. In fact, Mr. Voelcker was a witness at his marriage to Mrs. Faust. Recall the testimony from this honorable family, who were there at the time of the murder. Not one of the members of the Voelcker family could testify that Mr. Faust was there at the time the crime took place. Thank God for their honesty, because I will be the first to admit I would have believed any of the Voelckers if they said they saw Mr. Faust in the home committing this awful act … but they did not testify to that. Gentlemen, this leans heavily to reasonable doubt.

"And there is the issue of Isom Taylor, a black from Seguin, possibly angry that even though slavery ended and he is now free, the grass is not greener on the other side of the fence. You heard many respected gentlemen question his integrity. I may give him one or two benefits of a doubt, but when you have several issues questioning his integrity, it creates doubt. I would not hold much of this testimony heavily as I decided on whether or not to convict Mr. Faust.

"We also had the initial judge, Judge White, who presided at Mr. Faust's preliminary hearing, testify he no longer believes Isom Taylor's testimony. This is a judge, gentlemen, who has heard thousands of testimonials from hundreds of criminal cases throughout his twenty-five-year career.

"Furthermore, you had Dr. Lehde, who examined the alleged murder weapon. He could not make a 100 percent determination if the ax displayed as the murder weapon was in fact the murder weapon. He said it was possible, even though there are common axes that could inflict the same injuries to the victims. Now, gentlemen, if that does not bring doubt along with those other facts that I highlighted, then the justice system is broken. You as the jurors need to find this man not guilty as you look at these facts; it is unreasonable to listen to circumstances that the prosecution has given.

"And wait, gentlemen, there is more testimony that you must measure, and that is Detective Lyons. Again remember this was another desperate attempt to make an arrest in this high-profile case. The sheriff used his agents to talk to known criminals for statements against Mr. Faust. Gentlemen, if this is not desperation and does not create more doubt, then our justice system is failing. You have the power to make this right as a jury by rendering a true verdict.

"The key piece of testimony that should convince you Mr. Faust did not commit this crime is the testimony of the only witness and surviving victim of the crime who was inside the room where the crime took place. Mrs. Faust was assaulted by the assailant but said it was not her husband who committed this horrible crime.

"Let me repeat this, gentlemen. Mrs. Faust said it was not her husband who killed Emma Voelcker or injured her, causing permanent blindness. Gentlemen, this is crucial when it comes from not only the wife of the accused but the victim of the crime and the only true eyewitness who can establish this fact. Gentlemen of the jury, the prosecution has disputed these facts with no real evidence. I ask you to evaluate these facts of the case and find my client not guilty. Thank you for your continued attention on this most important case."

Judge Altgelt said, "Thank you, Captain Rust. Prosecutor Walker, you may begin."

Prosecutor Walker said, "Thank you, Your Honor. Gentlemen of the jury, I would not be standing here today if I did not believe that man"—he pointed at Faust—"is guilty of murdering Emma Voelcker. I say this because it is not simply my opinion, but my belief based on the facts of the case. I realize that the defense may have tried to portray the law in this case as desperate, but this is simply dedication to their sworn profession. There were numerous lawmen who lost days of sleep and did what we expect them to do—find the killer of our innocent child. These men and the community are dedicated to do everything in their power to ensure another child is not murdered in such a way.

"These lawmen have brought the accused, Mr. Faust, to face justice. He was brought in and not shot while he fled from law enforcement. These very same lawmen had to guard Mr. Faust to ensure his safety; this means the lawmen had to put their own lives at risk in the name of justice. Many have said they will take justice into their own hands by killing Mr. Faust, but our lawmen are here for one thing only: justice according to the laws of our land.

"The Voelckers have been through a lot, and they are honest people. We expect such honesty from all our witnesses the prosecution presented. Recall that the Voelckers were in attendance and were witnesses in Mr. Faust's marriage to Helen Faust. Which, by the way, the marriage was for less than a year. They testified they could not identify the murderer of their own child, but remember that they knew Faust. There were some important facts to consider, such as Mrs. Voelcker stating she suspected Mr. Faust as the murderer.

"Also remember there was no motive to kill a child or the possibility of a robbery that was interrupted. Valuables were left on the table in clear view under a dimly lit lamp. If the motive was robbery, not one single drawer was opened and not one valuable was taken, though the opportunity was there. Yes, let's talk of robbery as a motive. This was a robbery scheme to take what was left of the Rhodius inheritance, and it ended up in murder; Mr. Faust's motive was to kill his wife; you saw the injuries to Mrs. Faust.

"The attempt was there, and unfortunately there was a possible witness, young Emma Voelcker. Emma paid the price for the scheme that Mr. Faust orchestrated but failed in; his mistake was killing Emma Voelcker. His plan was to murder Mrs. Helen Faust, inherit her remaining inheritance, get a sympathy story, and convince Mrs. Rhodius he should marry her other daughter and take the final piece of the inheritance. Gentlemen, money is motive for many things, especially for murder. Mrs. Faust was clearly the target; there was no motive to kill Emma, and she was just silenced to conceal the crime. This is how evil men think. Mr. Faust is purely an evil man; he did not hesitate to kill a friend's dear child to get to the money he wanted to steal.

"The Voelckers also testified that the Fausts' dogs did not bark the entire time of the attack; however, they had to be removed when a stranger, who was the sheriff, arrived at the Voelcker home. This may seem like an odd point to bring out, but, gentlemen, we all are familiar with dogs. Dogs are obedient to their owners, and they pick up the scents of their owners. Do not think of this as a minor detail because the dogs were protective of Mrs. Faust. Yet they did not bark during the entire attack.

"Let's talk about Isom Taylor and why his testimony is valid and important to this case. First, Isom is simply a father who has one daughter, like many of us. Isom would not recklessly endanger himself or his family. He is a man of integrity doing the right thing, and that is what we should expect from every man. The sheriff of Guadalupe County, among many, said they would believe his testimony. What is not consistent is Judge White, who jailed Mr. Faust based on Isom Taylor's testimony yet does not believe him now and can state no reason for contradicting himself.

"Isom Taylor was simply fishing on the night of the murder and testified he knew who Mr. Faust was and recognized him, which puts Mr. Faust coming from New Braunfels right after the murder was committed. There was no testimony to account for why Faust went to the inn and not his home in Seguin. He has no alibi. His alibi cannot be substantiated by inn staff. There was no reason to stay there except to try to establish an alibi that fell apart.

"Furthermore, the murder weapon was found in the exact spot Isom Taylor testified to. This evidence of the crime begins to eliminate any doubt that Mr. Faust is the murderer. Dr. Lehde also found evidence of bone and blood from a mammal on the handle. Gentlemen, we use axes to cut wood, and there are tools to butcher animals; there should not be bone or blood on an ax.

"Gentlemen, if I may address the importance of Detective Lyons's investigation. Recall the Reno Brothers, a ruthless bunch of outlaws who got what they deserved. Well, these brothers once gave accurate information to lawmen and turned in two men who robbed a train, which had been blamed on the Reno Brothers' gang.

Gentlemen, information like this cannot be ignored, but it must be further verified, and it was verified with the testimony you heard at this trial. There is honor among thieves. As a prosecutor, I am well versed in this topic, I have never tried a case where a thief was witness against a fellow thief. Outlaws take care of their own problems, but deep down inside, these outlaws testified that Mr. Faust told them of his crimes. They said the motive behind the crime was to kill his wife. This clearly establishes the motive, which was murder for inheritance money he thought he could get. There was testimony that the murderer knew how to enter the home and knew where Mrs. Faust was sleeping. The outlaws who testified stated they have their own standards and do not accept child murderers as outlaws—they are cowards.

"We all have sympathy for Mrs. Faust and she indeed loves her husband, but she testified she was struck before she could see the attacker. This means she could not identify the attacker. This also means Faust could never be cleared as a suspect. Remember her own mother testified that she believed Faust was the murderer based on his desire to solicit their help to flee the law. These are not the actions of an innocent man; they are the actions of a guilty man. Gentlemen, I ask you to weigh the facts of the case and consider the pieces that connect the evidence of testimony given that find Mr. Faust guilty of the murder of young Emma Voelcker. Thank you, gentlemen."

Judge Altgelt turned to the jury and instructed them, "Members of the jury, you will deliberate until a verdict is rendered. It is your duty to determine guilt or innocence. I will decide the punishment if you render a guilty verdict. A guilty verdict must be unanimous. Bailiff, escort the jury to the jury room and remain outside until the jury foreman advises they are ready."

The bailiff called out, "All rise!" and the jury followed the bailiff to the jury room to deliberate.

• •

In the jury room, discussion immediately commenced about a verdict. Franz Nowotny was quiet and observed the jurors discussing issues about the case. There were some who agreed on Mr. Faust being guilty, while others disagreed. After a good thirty minutes, the disagreements became more provocative, and Franz Nowotny spoke.

"Gentlemen, I suggest we start with where we are at right now so we can agree or agree to disagree. Let's go around the table and see if we have anything close to a verdict."

Henry Dirks said, "Guilty."

Adolph Penshorn said, "Guilty."

H. W. Boehm said, "Not guilty."

Wenzel Nowotny said, "Not guilty."

John Marschall said, "Not guilty."

Joseph Pfeiffer said, "Guilty."

Andreas Pape said, "Guilty."

Peter Nowotny said, "Guilty."

Christian Guenther said, "Not guilty."

Peter Daum said, "Guilty."

Max Tausch said, "Guilty."

Franz Nowotny said, "I say guilty … Well, we have four who say not guilty and the rest say guilty. Now we all know each other; some of us are related. I was a law student before the war, and I never finished. Justice is blind, and wherever the scales tip with the most weight is where the law sides. I say we point out the most important five pieces of evidence presented and discuss and agree if the evidence is valid enough for guilt. If three or more lands for guilty or not guilty, then we all agree we will vote that way, do you all agree?"

All the jurors looked at each other and agreed that this was the way it was going to be.

Adolph Penshorn said, "Well, let's get started. An anxious town waits for our decision."

Franz said, "Let's talk about the five pieces of evidence. The first piece is the ax; the second is testimony of the living victim, Mrs. Faust; the third is the confession obtained by Detective Lyons from the outlaws; the fourth is the testimony of the mother of Mrs. Faust, Mrs. Rhodius; and the fifth piece is the testimony of Isom Taylor."

Franz continued, "Now I will ask each of you about each piece of evidence, and we will say it is either yay or nay whether the evidence is valid enough to convict Mr. Faust. The first part is the ax presented as evidence. Did the prosecutor make their case convincing you this was evidence showing Mr. Faust's guilt? One at a time, let's vote."

Henry Dirks said, "Nay."

Adolph Penshorn said, "Nay."

H. W. Boehm said, "Yay."

Wenzel Nowotny said, "Nay."

John Marschall said, "Yay."

Joseph Pfeiffer said, "Nay."

Andreas Pape said, "Nay; the doctor said it may have been but didn't seem sure."

Peter Nowotny said, "Yay."

Christian Guenther said, "Nay."

Peter Daum said, "Nay."

Max Tausch said, "Nay."

Franz said, "I say nay; it may have been used, but there are enough doubts. So that is one vote to not convict Mr. Faust. Next piece of evidence is the testimony of Mrs. Faust—do we believe her? Let's vote."

Henry Dirks said, "Yay."

Adolph Penshorn said, "Yay."

H. W. Boehm said, "Yay."

Wenzel Nowotny said, "Yay."

John Marschall said, "Nay."

Joseph Pfeiffer said, "Yay."

Andreas Pape said, "Nay."

Peter Nowotny said, "Yay."

Christian Guenther said, "Nay."

Peter Daum said, "Yay."

Max Tausch said, "Yay."

Franz said, "I say yay. I think most of us agree we believe she did not see him. We may think he did it, but I know you all are thinking the same thing. Nobody in that house where the murder was committed can say they saw him—that is two for the defense. I guess one more, and we will have our verdict. Now to the next issue, Detective Lyons's confession obtained from the outlaws."

Henry Dirks said, "Yay."

Adolph Penshorn said, "Yay."

H. W. Boehm said, "Yay."

Wenzel Nowotny said, "Yay."

John Marschall said, "Nay."

Joseph Pfeiffer said, "Yay."

Andreas Pape said, "Nay."

Peter Nowotny said, "Yay."

Christian Guenther said, "Nay."

Peter Daum said, "Yay."

Max Tausch said, "Yay."

Franz said, "I say yay; that detective was sharp. He had no reason to lie, and we know there have been codes of honor even among thieves. That is one for the prosecution. Now next is the issue of Mrs. Rhodius, the mother of Helen Faust. Let's decide on this issue."

Henry Dirks said, "Yay."

Adolph Penshorn said, "Yay."

H. W. Boehm said, "Yay."

Wenzel Nowotny said, "Yay."

John Marschall said, "Nay."

Joseph Pfeiffer said, "Yay."

Andreas Pape said, "Nay."

Peter Nowotny said, "Yay."

Christian Guenther said, "Nay."

Peter Daum said, "Yay."

Max Tausch said, "Yay."

Franz said, "I say yay; a mother knows her children. Now we are tied two and two. The next piece of evidence is from the Negro man, Isom Taylor. Let's vote."

The jurors got quiet, and one by one they looked at each other. Franz said, "Look, I know what some of you may be thinking. We are the judges here; some of us fought our own, and many of us know many who died. Our country fought over this issue to have a right to a trial by jury. It took this to decide over slavery. We are mostly German immigrants and were hated by the locals until we integrated and became united. We unknowingly got pushed to pick a side for this war that we did not want. The former slaves were here before us and had been waiting for freedom. I am not trying to influence you, but my vote is yay, I believe him like any other honest man. Let's get this done. What do you all think?"

Henry Dirks said, "Yay."

Adolph Penshorn said, "Yay."

H. W. Boehm said, "Yay."

Wenzel Nowotny said, "Yay."

John Marschall said, "Yay."

Joseph Pfeiffer said, "Yay."

Andreas Pape said, "Yay."

Peter Nowotny said, "Yay."

Christian Guenther said, "Yay."

Peter Daum said, "Yay."

Max Tausch said, "Yay."

Franz said, "Let's do our duty. I will let the bailiff know we have come to a decision. Bailiff."

The bailiff came in and said, "Yes, sir?"

Franz said, "Bailiff, inform the judge we have a verdict."

The bailiff said, "Are you all sure? That was awfully fast."

Franz nodded his head.

CHAPTER 14

THE VERDICT AND THE SENTENCE

The bailiff went across the street to the courthouse and found Judge Altgelt, who ordered the bailiff to find Prosecutor Walker and Captain Rust.

The crowd assembled outside the courthouse began to flood the courtroom, anticipating the reading of the verdict. The judge went to the bench to sit down, and Prosecutor Walker entered and sat at the prosecutor's table. Captain Rust came in, and the deputies brought in Mr. Faust, who was seated next to Captain Rust.

Captain Rust said to Mr. Faust, "Now no matter what happens, do not show any emotion. If you're found not guilty, people are going to be unhappy; if you are found guilty, we will appeal this to the Supreme Court."

Mr. Faust nodded his head, and the judge saw that everyone except the jury was in the courtroom.

Judge Altgelt said to the bailiff, "Bring in the jury."

The jury was escorted in, and all eyes were on the jury after the judge ordered everyone seated. The judge said, "Now as the verdict is read, there will be absolutely no outburst from anyone. Mr. Foreman, have you all reached a verdict?"

Franz said, "Yes, Your Honor, we have."

Judge Altgelt said, "Bailiff, collect the verdict from the foreman."

Franz handed a paper to the judge, and the judge said, "Captain Rust and Mr. Faust, please stand as I read the verdict."

Captain Rust and Mr. Faust stood up.

Judge Altgelt said, "For the charge of murder of the first degree, I find you guilty."

The courtroom cheered, and some wept tears. The judge again demanded order.

The judge looked at the courtroom, which quieted once again, and said, "William Faust, I sentence you to a term of life in prison."

The courtroom erupted in chaos; the judge demanded order, but the uproar was too loud. Sheriff Saur yelled frantically for the crowd to calm, but nobody listened. People shouted, "Hang him, hang him!"

Suddenly, a thunderous shot was fired, and the crowd became silent in fear. Sheriff Saur had just fired his pistol and declared, "Court is over; everyone out."

The crowd slowly dispersed but was still filled with the energy of dismay and anger.

Sheriff Saur said, "We have to escort Mr. Faust out. The crowd is going to kill him. Get to the jail."

Sheriff Saur gathered four of his deputies, including Deputy Schmidt. Sheriff Saur said to Detective Lyons, "Ask the city marshal for his help in controlling the crowd outside."

Deputy Schmidt checked the back, and he and Sheriff Saur grabbed Faust and took him quickly to the county jail.

Sheriff Saur said, "I have got to control this crowd. When I leave, do not let anyone in. I will send Deputy Schultz to help you. Switch shifts with him and stay here through the night; I will talk to the crowd."

Sheriff Saur walked behind the upset crowd and fired his pistol in the air. The crowd turned to him.

Sheriff Saur said, "This trial is over for today. Now you all go on home."

A voice from the crowd yelled, "No justice; hang Faust!"

The sheriff fired his pistol in the air again and said, "The judge said there will be no hanging. He is the law, and I will enforce it. Anyone who attempts to kill Faust will be treated like any other murderer."

The crowd was dismayed and began to chatter bitterly as they started to disperse. The sight of the city marshal and his posse approaching convinced the crowd to disperse even faster. City Marshal Kellner rode next to the sheriff and said, "Sheriff, we are here to assist. This is probably going to be a long night."

Sheriff Saur said, "Much obliged. I do not disagree with the crowd, but we have to uphold the law and protect that son of a bitch."

Marshal Emil Kellner said, "I thought they would hang him for sure, and I thought the jury would take a while to decide. Sorry I am late."

Sheriff Saur said, "I am most obliged you are here. Let's meet at the jail."

Sheriff Saur had ten deputies at the jail, and Marshal Kellner had seven, including himself.

Sheriff Saur said, "I need five out front; the rest come on inside."

Once inside, the posse of town marshals and deputy sheriffs filled the room. The jail had five cells inside, and William Faust was the only one chained to his bunk. He could hear everything that would be said at this meeting.

Sheriff Saur said, "I need four men posted at this jail at all hours of the day and night."

Marshal Kellner said, "You guys need some rest. My posse will take care of tonight. Relieve us in the morning."

Sheriff Saur said, "You know I appreciate that, and you are right. We are exhausted from guarding the jurors and Isom Taylor's family. My men could use the rest."

Marshal Kellner said, "We will get it from here; you all go home. Sheriff, I know you are nearby, and if you hear shots, I know you will be coming."

Sheriff Saur said, "We will be in after dawn. Thank you." Sheriff Saur looked at his deputies and said, "We will be ready to go in the morning."

There was a knock at the door, and the lawmen jumped. The sheriff nodded to the deputy to open the door. It was a young man in his early twenties.

Sheriff Saur told him, "You can't be here. Nobody can be here tonight. Is there something that needs my immediate attention?"

The young man was a tall, slender fellow who took his hat off and said, "My name is Arnold, and I have ridden all the way from La Vaca County. My father was killed by a man named Faust after he robbed him of all we had. I was there and will never forget his face. Can I see him?"

Sheriff Saur asked, "Are you armed, boy?"

Arnold answered, "No."

Sheriff Saur let him in and pointed at Faust. "Is that him?"

Arnold stared at Faust, who looked at the boy and quickly looked away.

Arnold said, "That is him. He needs to be charged for my father's murder."

Faust said, "My brother killed your father. If it is satisfying to you, he died five years ago."

Arnold said, "No, it was you. I know you recognize me, and I never forgot your face."

The sheriff looked at Mr. Faust and told Arnold, "I do not have jurisdiction to investigate him for that murder in this county. Let the sheriff of your town know."

Arnold said, "What will happen to him?"

Sheriff Saur said, "Well, if there is enough evidence, he will go to trial."

Arnold said, "So he can get life? That is the easy way out … Thank you, Sheriff. I will take care of it the way you said."

After the young man left, Sheriff Saur said, "I wonder how many he has killed." He turned to Faust and asked, "Would you tell us, William?"

Faust did not respond and looked away from the lawman staring at him.

CHAPTER 15

TENSIONS RISE IN THE TOWN

It was now after eight o'clock, and the sun was down. Mr. Faust did not eat; he sat on his bunk smoking a cigar.

Mr. Faust said, "Marshal, I can see through some of these holes in the wall, and this window above my bunk is no good."

Marshal Kellner was playing cards with his deputy marshals and said, "Well, if you are thinking about breaking out, the town will kill you, not us. So don't do it."

Mr. Faust said, "I know my life for whatever it is worth now is in your hands, Marshal."

At 10:30 p.m., the town had been quiet for a while, and Mr. Faust was asleep. The deputies started to hear shots in the distance, and Mr. Faust awakened. The deputy marshals put their cards down and pulled their rifles close. The two deputy marshals posted outside checked in with the marshal.

Deputy Marshal Jenkins said, "We are going to take a look and will be right back."

The deputy marshals began to play cards again, and Faust went back to sleep. Shots in the distance could be heard again toward the east. The deputy marshals were alerted once again, and this time they could hear a thunderous noise that broke the silence of the town after 11:00 p.m. It was a lot of horses at full gallop approaching from the west. The marshal was there with two deputy marshals inside. Faust was chained to the wall on his bunk.

About eight men on horseback, wearing burlap hoods and holding torches, ropes, and rifles, converged on the jail. The leader yelled to bring out Faust or the place would burn.

The marshal shouted back, "We are many, and that is not going to happen!"

Suddenly, a rock broke through the window, and the marshals were forced to take cover as gunfire engulfed the jail from all directions. It was cover fire as one of the lynch men tied a rope to his horse and tied it to the jail door, ripping it off. The marshals were pinned down, and the lynch mob stormed the jail. They held the marshal and his deputies at gunpoint and ripped the keys from one of the deputy marshals' belt. Faust stood there on the bed; all he could do was stare and accept whatever was going to take place. Faust knew they were there to hang him. Three lynch men opened Faust's cell. Two men tried to pull him off the bunk while he was still chained to the wall. The third man tried to unlock the restraints with the keys. Suddenly, a shotgun blast froze everyone. The sheriff was at the door, pointing his pistol at the men in Faust's cell.

Sheriff Saur said, "Leave him be, or you will be the ones staying in that cell."

The leader of the lynch mob had the marshals on the floor at gunpoint and said, "Boys, let's go; we will be back. Marshal, we are leaving; we won't shoot if you don't."

The sheriff looked at the marshal, who was helpless, with his hands up and facing the barrel of a six-shooter. He said, "All right, get your men and get out of here. You men are now outlaws for what you just did. I will find you."

The hooded men immediately left and rode off into the night, leaving their torches and disappearing quickly into darkness.

Sheriff Saur said, "Marshals, are you all right?"

Marshal Kellner was rubbing the back of his head, realizing that he had been hit with the butt of a rifle, and said, "Sorry about that, Sheriff. They came in quickly. They planned the diversion and the break-in."

Sheriff Saur looked around and said, "We cannot defend the jail; it is small and falling apart. We will move Faust to the courthouse and arrange to get him moved to San Antonio until his appeal."

The sheriff and the marshal began taking the restraints off Faust, and the marshals quickly took him over to the courthouse.

Sheriff Saur said, "I believe that lynch mob will grow in numbers. Was anyone able to recognize anyone?"

The deputy marshals and the marshal looked at each other, and Marshal Kellner said, "No, we did not recognize any of them."

Sheriff Saur said, "Place Faust in the holding cell in the courthouse. Put some men on the roof and outside. At least three inside."

Sheriff Saur looked at the window in the courtroom cell. It was small, but a person passing by could see Faust in his bunk.

Sheriff Saur said, "Post someone outside that window at all times."

When the first night was over, it was the weekend. The officials in San Antonio would not be available until at least Monday. Faust and the sheriff's posse would be stuck together for perhaps a long weekend.

• •

Day Two after the Trial

There were no significant occurrences throughout the day. The night was rough for the deputies. Every hour a rider on horseback would gallop past the courthouse and fire several shots through the air to awaken the deputies and spot their positions.

The next morning, Sheriff Saur came in and relieved Deputy Schmidt. Sheriff Saur asked, "Everyone all good? Anything we should worry about?"

Deputy Schmidt was exhausted and said, "Nobody slept all night. Riders came through every hour all through the night."

Sheriff Saur said, "We need to hold them off till Monday morning."

Deputy Schmidt told him, "They're doing a good job of probing us, like the Comanches. Before they attacked, they would mess with us for nights in the camps and sneak in with no resistance past tired soldiers and do some damage."

• •

Day Three after the Trial

Day three was quiet; twelve men total stood guard. The sun went down, and the town was a ghost town. The town was usually occupied with men drinking at the saloons or coming in late to stay at the hotel, but tonight the town was empty. It was near eleven o'clock. A lot of the men had fallen asleep and started to take turns at 50 percent security: six were asleep, while the other six were on guard.

At 1:00 a.m. gunshots could be heard again. The shots

were continuous, and the sheriff said, "I think the lynch mob is coming again. I am going to confront them before they get here and put a stop to it."

Sheriff Saur took six men with him and rode toward the gunfire. Sheriff Saur and the six men could see a large group of riders with glowing torches. They were stationary, not moving toward the town.

The riders noticed the sheriff and stopped firing their guns. The sheriff told the other riders to stay and watch his back while he communicated with the leader.

Sheriff Saur yelled, "Who is in charge here?"

Nobody answered the sheriff; the hooded group did not want their voices to be recognized. Finally, a man in the group said, "I am."

Sheriff Saur said, "I would be willing to bet that all of you are decent people and not outlaws, I feel the same way you do about Faust. Even if you do not believe in the law, revenge is in the eye of the beholder."

The unidentified man said, "Sheriff, all we want is Faust. There is no reason why he should be alive. The judge should have hung him."

The mob started to yell in agreement with the leader of the group.

The sheriff noticed that he was no longer able to see the courthouse; he was around a bend from it.

The leader turned, looked at the mob, and said, "I know this sheriff. He is a good man, but he will make each and every one of us answer if we go any further." The masked leader added, "Let's go home, boys."

The rest of the mob yelled and turned away from town, firing off hundreds of rounds in the air as they rode in the opposite direction from town.

Deputy Schmidt said, "That was a little too easy. I thought there would be a fight for sure."

Sheriff Saur said, "Well, they are still suited up for battle, and the night is still young. This is not over yet."

The six men rode back into town, and Deputy Schmidt saw a slender male walking away from the courthouse.

Deputy Schmidt said, "That looks like that Arnold fellow who said Faust shot his father."

Sheriff Saur concurred. "It sure does look like him."

The deputies left at the courthouse said, "Sheriff, are you all okay? We heard the shots from all over the place and thought you all were dead."

Sheriff Saur replied, "No, it was a group of about twenty-five men, and they said they would leave, but they still may be out there."

The sheriff then said, "Let's go inside and get ready in case they come back."

Sheriff Saur and Deputy Schmidt went to check on Faust, and he was asleep on the bunk facedown.

Deputy Schmidt shouted, "Open the door!"

A deputy came in and opened the door, and Deputy Schmidt turned Faust over. He was shot in his back and the back of his head. Faust was dead.

Sheriff Saur looked at the window and said, "Boys, they fooled us. The mob was a distraction. When they fired the shots, that was their signal. They are not coming back. Quick, you all search the town; pick up anyone you see. If you find young Arnold, bring him here."

After nearly thirty minutes, the sheriff's posse came back in from searching the town. It was quiet, and nobody had been found.

Young Arnold hid near the Guadalupe, and at sunrise he started to ride back to La Vaca. He noticed the town of New

Braunfels light up with the sunrise. He made the sign of the cross and tilted his hat toward New Braunfels. Then he rode off back home to La Vaca.

• •

The city of New Bruanfels would eventually return to a normal state. The town would always remember the beautiful, young Emma Voelcker, who was brutally murdered. The Rhodius family would bury William Faust in their family cemetery at the pleading of his loyal wife, Helen Faust. The actual murder of William Faust was never solved. He was suspected of at least two other murders, the father of Arnold and a Dr. Rhein.

Special thanks to the New Braunfels
Herald-Zeitung

Printed in the United States
By Bookmasters